THE FAR-FARERS

Other titles in this series

THE FAR-FARERS

CHRIS SAVERY

LUTTERWORTH PRESS · LONDON

First paperback edition 1972

ISBN 0 7188 1945 4

COPYRIGHT © 1960 LUTTERWORTH PRESS

*Printed in Great Britain
by Fletcher & Son Ltd, Norwich*

CONTENTS

Faro their vida um Island at boda Guds ord

Far fared they round Iceland to preach the
Word of God

Thorvald's Saga

Chapter 1

THE LOST LETTER

THE taxi halted beside a number 11 bus and waited for the traffic lights to change colour. It was at that moment that Peter's father discovered that the letter was not in his pocket. He showed signs of annoyance, breathing deeply through his nose.

"Try another pocket," suggested Peter.

"If I have told you once, my boy, I have mentioned a thousand times that I always keep things in their proper places. I am a man of method. This is the only pocket to be used for letters."

The taxi swept over the crossing and Peter kept his eyes on the car in front, saying nothing, which was the only thing to say.

His father inspected once again the contents of his letter pocket. They were few in number, for the pockets of Royal Air Force best blue uniform are not improved by being used as storage dumps. With a grunt, Squadron Leader Porter admitted defeat and began to turn out his other pockets. The letter was in none of them. Peter Porter looked straight ahead. It was wisest so to do.

"I have lost the wretched letter," growled his

father, as the taxi turned down the slope which leads towards the departure platforms of Liverpool Street Station. "Have you been up to mischief hiding it?"

"No, of course not, Father. I am not such a lunatic as to hide the letter which tells where I am to go. You must have dropped it somewhere."

The taxi drew up and the driver glared at his passengers. They were hunting frantically in all the pockets of both their coats.

"Peter, what was Mavis doing when you said good-bye?"

"She was sailing paper boats in the bath, making them out of the corners of an old envelope, the way you showed her the other day. . . . Oh, Dad! You don't think she tore up that letter, do you?"

"Make it snappy, sir," said the taxi-driver.

Squadron Leader Porter paid his fare without so much as glancing at the indicator to check its accuracy, an unheard-of omission, which showed how distraught his mind was.

"I'll give that girl a hiding when I get home. . . ."

"No, you won't, Dad. She's only four and she can't read yet. Besides, it was your fault. You sent her away from the breakfast table for spilling my tea into my porridge, and the poor kid amused herself by doing what you yourself had taught her."

"Well, what are we going to do now?"

They stood together in the great booking hall, while Squadron Leader Porter racked his brains to remember the contents of the letter which he had glanced at, but barely read through, when it arrived by the morning post.

"Your uncle said that he and all the family are down with chickenpox, so you cannot go to them just yet. He has arranged for you to join a party of schoolboys going for a cruise on the Broads. Their school is having staggered holidays to avoid the August crush."

"Uncle Bill wrote all that in the letter which came yesterday. Today's letter must have said where the cruise starts from."

"Of course, of course. I would have read the letter aloud if you had not made such a fuss about a splash of tea in your porridge. You must take things calmly, my boy."

"It wasn't a splash of tea, it was a flood, and porridge with tea tastes awful! What about my railway ticket, Dad? Where am I going?"

Squadron Leader Porter clutched his chin, a sure sign of irritability. All around them travellers walked purposefully, knowing exactly their destinations. It was most vexatious to be obliged to admit that he simply did not know where Peter was to go.

"If Uncle Bill was on the phone we could ring him up."

"Don't talk nonsense, Peter. You know very well he is not on the phone. A telegram would be useless, for I must return at once to collect Mother and the children. I could not wait for a reply."

"It must be some place in the east of England. The Broads are in Norfolk, aren't they?"

"Wroxham? Ranworth? Potter Heigham? Oulton Broad? No, I believe you were to meet somebody at Ely, yes, Ely. Ah! Now I have it! You were to meet a bearded man at Ely, the schoolmaster in command I gather."

"A schoolmaster with a beard at Ely. O.K. Dad. What was his name?"

The name of the bearded man had gone beyond recall and the next train for Ely was due out in three minutes time.

"I haven't the faintest notion. Ely is a small town and there cannot be above twenty beards at most in the place. It is hardly likely that more than one of the twenty will be conducting a cruise for schoolboys on the Broads. You've a tongue in your head, son. Find the most respectable beard— here's your ticket—the most schoolmasterly beard, and ask him if he is the chap. Don't lose the ticket. . . . Mind you don't go off with any poor type. . . . I trust I have brought you up with enough sense to judge for yourself . . . run, lad, over the bridge. . . . If there's any difficulty, ring up Squadron Leader Frost at Fenpool R.A.F. Station and ask if you can stay with them till Uncle Bill's family is out of quarantine. . . . He's an old pal of mine. Fenpool's somewhere near Ely. Tell him I'm posted to Singapore and have got the wonderful chance of flying Mother and the babies in my aircraft instead of leaving them to follow.

Mother will need my help going all the way to Singapore with the twins nine months and Mavis, who needs a bodyguard just for herself alone."

Peter followed his father to the train with a shrug of his shoulders. In his estimation, Mother was quite capable of escorting as many babies as had the old woman in the shoe to Singapore, or to the moon if need be. Dad might be first class as regards aeroplane engines, but he'd be more trouble on a journey than twenty babies. Good old Dad!

"Here's a comfortable carriage for you with a window seat. You've got enough pocket money? Uncle Bill will give you more after the holidays. Have a good time on the Broads, sailing, swimming, fishing. Work hard at school, son. Play the game and all that. Two years will soon pass and we'll all be back again. My love to Aunt Eva and the kids. It's a jolly family, as you know, so you'll be as happy as a sandboy, whatever a sandboy may be! Cheerio, Peter! Look out for the bearded man at Ely. All the best!"

The train steamed out and Peter waved until he could see Dad's ginger head and blue uniform no longer. Then with a sinking feeling inside he sat down in his corner seat.

"Pull up the window, young man," snapped the little old lady opposite. He pulled it up.

"May I lend you a handkerchief to wipe your tears away? 'Parting is such sweet sorrow', as the poet said."

" No, thanks." Peter drew himself up stiffly, and stared out of the window. He did not like the look of the queer old lady who sat swinging her feet which did not reach the floor. She wore dark glasses and her dress was faded to a mouldy green. Bits of black glass jingled in her bonnet. She was the most old-fashioned article that a museum could produce.

"A peppermint humbug might calm the emotions." She fumbled in her aged handbag and produced a sticky mess of melted sweets with a paper bag disintegrating about them. Peter declined her offer and buried himself in a Wild West story which he had brought with him.

The old lady, discouraged, peered at him through her heavy glasses, examining his luggage, and pursing up her lips as if in scorn. Then she turned her attention to the other occupants of the carriage; teasing a fat baby, arguing with its mother, scolding a man who produced a pipe in a non-smoking carriage, criticizing the over-red lipstick worn by a smart girl. It was not a pleasant journey. The baby howled. Its mother wept. The man put away his pipe, but he took a pinch of snuff in such a noisy manner that the smart girl giggled. The old lady sucked her rejected peppermints till the carriage reeked of them and then produced an orange into which she stuffed a lump of sugar. Her swinging feet kicked Peter on the shins but she did not apologize.

He was glad when they came to Ely. The wide

platform was almost empty. There was a group of airmen, a couple of farmers in leather gaiters and there, standing by the bookstall watching the incoming train, was the man who had come to meet him, a young man in a huge duffle coat. He had a thick golden beard and he was accompanied by a magnificent husky pup. Peter studied the man carefully as he waited for his fellow-travellers to get out first. Yes, he looked eminently respectable, though a bit warmly dressed for the end of June. Judging by his beard and his dog, one would imagine that he was a young naval officer, just back from a journey to the Antarctic. He was not in the least like the masters at Peter's school, but he was certainly what Dad would consider a good type.

"Good morning, sir," said Peter Porter. "Are you expecting a boy to join your cruise?"

The man grinned and the dog pricked up its ears.

"So you are the chap, are you? Glad to make your acquaintance. I'm Jim James."

"I'm Peter Porter, sir."

"You needn't sir me. I'm Jim. That all your luggage? Sent the rest in advance did you? Well, I expect you have enough in that bag. Come here, Cherry-Garrard!"

"What a funny name for a dog. Why do you call him Cherry-Garrard?"

"In memory of the explorer Cherry-Garrard, who made 'the worst journey in the world' to find the eggs of the Emperor penguin and didn't even get a 'Thank you' when he took them along to present them to a museum. It's my way of showing gratitude to a bloke who suffered for the cause of science. I intend to give C-G to a lad on our trip whose home is in Iceland, just the country for a husky. He's not really tameable."

He swung open the door of a small sports car and heaved Peter on top of a pile of luggage in the back seat. Cherry-Garrard, his fierce little eyes gleaming with pride and independence, took the place by the driver as his right. Jim James was about to drive off when there was a yell behind the car:

"Stop! Hey there! Stop!"

For a moment Peter thought the shout was addressed to him. Then he saw that it was meant for the old lady from the train, who came running down the road, her bonnet jingling, and her roughly furled umbrella waving. She was screaming remarks over her shoulder as she ran, but Peter could not distinguish what she said. An elderly man was running after her, with a look of determination, as if intent on murdering the old girl. A couple of porters from the railway station joined in the chase, and the clerk from the booking-office came out to see the fun. Jim James laughed and drove off the other way, so they did not see the end of the chase. Peter felt he hardly cared what became of the objectionable old lady, but he was definitely worried about the man, for he sported a neat black beard.

Jim James and his husky dog did not look like a schoolmaster, and the other fellow did, but no schoolmaster on earth would chase a peculiar old lady through the streets of a quiet cathedral town. Such ungallant behaviour proved beyond all doubt that Blackbeard was a poor type.

"There's a harmonica among the junk you are sitting on," said Jim. "Unpack it and play a tune if you are musically inclined. You may find the drive a bit boring. We are going to Lowestoft via Newmarket, Bury St. Edmunds, and Oulton Broad."

There was a harmonica, an accordion, a fiddle and a flute in the back, but Peter was not musically inclined. He wanted to find out about the journey.

"Do we start the cruise at Oulton Broad?"

"No. At Lowestoft. You'll meet the rest of the crowd on the boat. I expected to pick up one chap at the other place, but he wired to say he'd be on the docks tonight."

"What other place?"

"Cambridge of course. It's not far from Ely, an awful hole I've heard. I'm Oxford myself, of course."

"I thought you were in the Navy."

"That's on account of my beard. A handsome growth, isn't it? But I'm not a Navy man, only a poor scholar of Teddy Hall. Ever heard of it, Peter Porter?"

He chatted on about undergraduate life at St. Edmund's Hall, Oxford, which seemed mostly

composed of rags, punting on the river, and avoiding the proctors. From that Jim James went on to
talk of space travel and music and old churches.
He talked most of all about old churches in East
Anglia, and stopped several times to point out flint
knapping, and odd rounded towers built apart
from the main church. They got out to inspect
hammer-beam angels on the roof of one small
country church, and old stained glass in another,
the real mediæval blue which Jim James declared
could never be reproduced by modern craftsmen,
in spite of all their scientific knowledge.

Peter thought hungrily of the lunch he had
missed, but one could not show greed the very first
day of the cruise. Jim James was so delighted
about his old churches that Peter felt infected with
an interest he had never felt before. In fact he had
hardly ever been inside a church. They did not
take that line in the Porter family.

"Bungay, now, that's an interesting church.
You must see it. A ghost dog appeared once, they
say, in the middle of a service, and terrified the
congregation. Black as coal he was, with fire coming out of his mouth. I don't know whether there's
any truth in the tale, but they still talk of the
Black Dog of Bungay. We'll have a spot of tea at
Bungay."

Good! Peter was quite ready for tea long before
they reached Bungay, but a hasty meal of one shiny
bun and a cup of tea was all he had time for. Jim
was in a hurry to drive on.

"We must get to Lowestoft in time. I've been too long on the road already, but East Anglia is a wonderful country for churches. I'm hoping to be a clergyman some day, so I cannot help being thrilled when I see a church. Hurry up or we shall not arrive before the *Far-Farer* sets sail."

"*Far-Farer*, is that the name of the cruiser?"

"Well, I'd hardly call her a cruiser, you know. She's just a right little, tight little Lowestoft trawler. We've hired her for our cruise, and we've changed her name among ourselves, though she's still by rights the *Gladys Lee*. We call her the *Far-Farer*, because we are going to fare far in her, and we call ourselves, the ship's company, 'the far-farers'. You are now a far-farer, Peter Porter. By the way, why do you call yourself that?"

"I dunno. Suppose my parents liked the name Peter. Tell me about the ship. I thought she'd be a cabin cruiser. I've heard of people going on the Broads in cabin cruisers."

"Drifters, smacks, trawlers, yawls, you'll see all sorts in Lowestoft harbour. I'm not much of a seaman, so I'll leave skipper to explain her workings. He'll yarn for hours about mackerel, herrings and halibut."

"What's it like on the Broads?"

"The Broads? Oh, they're fine. We'll be coming up to Oulton Broad soon. George Borrow lived there once. That's where he wrote *Lavengro* and *Romany Rye*. 'Life is sweet, brother', you

B

know the quotation, ' there's likewise a wind on the heath ' . . . I forget how it goes."

He rambled on about gipsies and that led him to something else, and away to another subject, and Peter sat on the pile of rugs and clothing, surrounded by musical instruments, staring at the scenery and thinking of Mother and Father and the kids. They must have taken off for Singapore by now. What adventures they would have! Even little Mavis would see more of the world than her brother. A trip on the Broads sounded deadly dull, cooped up in a trawler with a crowd of school-boys who knew one another but didn't know him, or want to either. They would sail for days between level banks where grey willow trees grew and solemn cows looked down through sedges. Perhaps some idiot would fall into the water and have to be rescued. Maybe they would play cricket in a field or go fishing. Mum and Dad were flying half round the world, but Peter was to call himself a far-farer, and fare no farther than the waterways of East Anglia. And when the cruise was over, he would join his cousins and go to their dull school for two dreary years. Uncle Bill and Aunt Eva were quite passable, but not a patch on Mother and Father.

" I hope you won't feel homesick," boomed the voice of Jim James, breaking in on Peter's reverie. " At least I have now told you the plan and pur-pose of our trip, so you know what to expect. I hope you'll be happy among the far-farers."

Peter Porter swallowed hard. The lump in his throat prevented him from explaining that he had not been listening to the bearded man's pleasant chatter for the last half hour and so had completely missed the explanations and plans of which he spoke. They were driving past Oulton Broad now, all crowded with motor cruisers and sailing boats, yachts and wherries. And so they came to Lowestoft, a busy town which smelt strongly of fish.

Chapter 2

TWELVE FISHERMEN

"HELLO, mates! This is the chap I wrote about. Has Doc given you the gen about him?"

Jim James shoved Peter into the small cabin and he faced eleven pairs of eyes all looking at him as if he were a strange fish drawn up in a net.

"They know what line to take," said a chubby young man who was arranging bottles and bandages in a First Aid box with a red cross painted on it. "I have explained the treatment advised by psychiatry for cases of split-mind or schizophrenia, so we are prepared for any emergency."

Peter could not follow what seemed to be meant as a joke. However he smiled feebly in an effort to show politeness. His mind felt split certainly and he could not think of anything to say, for among the whole crowd there was not one who could be described with accuracy as a schoolboy. They were all dressed like fishermen, some in heavy blue woollen sweaters, others in rust-coloured jerkins, like those worn by the men on the trawlers he had noticed as they came up to the jetty. One was quite old, the skipper, no doubt. He had a fringe of white hair round his shiny bald head, white whiskers and gold ear-rings. On the top bunk sat a foreign-looking youth, fair-haired and blue-eyed, like a Norwegian or Dane. He wasn't more than sixteen, perhaps. All the others were twenty at least. This was no schoolboy cruise at all.

"Introduce yourself, my boy, and then we shall know who you claim to be," said a man with a commanding air who sat at the head of the table. He was a person who meant to be obeyed.

"I am Peter Porter," said Peter.

"That's what you call yourself, is it? Where do you come from?"

"From Nottingham. My father is in the R.A.F. and he has been posted to Singapore. The relations I was going to stay with have all got chicken-pox and I have not had it, so my uncle arranged that I should come for a cruise with you until they are out of quarantine."

The dark-eyed fellow on Peter's right whistled softly. The man at the head of the table raised his eyebrows.

"Well, according to our medical man, we ought not to argue, so we will leave your story there. Now listen to this. We will nickname you Ingolf, after the first Norse settler in Iceland. You understand that is a nickname only. We do not make up fairy tales on this trip. We prefer the truth."

Peter opened his mouth to explain that he had been telling the truth, but the words did not come.

Jim James gave him an encouraging bang on the shoulder.

"Welcome to the noble company of the far-farers, Ingolf, my bold sea-rover. Let me now introduce the others to you. Myself you already know; I am the most important, because it was from my fertile brain that the idea of this cruise sprang. On my right is David, the sweet singer of Israel, only it's his violin that he's best at, that fiddle you were sitting next to in the car. On your left, Ingolf, is David's special friend, Taffy from Wales, coal-miner, tenor, the best fellow in the world. Beyond him you see Doc, the fellow with the bottles. He has already marked you down as suffering from a disease with a long name, so be careful about playing any practical jokes. Doc is a medical student, so he will look after our health, up to page six hundred in the Family Doctor's Book, which is as far as he's got."

Jim James paused for breath and then started up again :

"The Rev. Robert is really the head of our company, being a parson, curate in a dockside parish, so he knows something of the water. The guy with the white whiskers is our skipper, Captain Dan May, whose fishing vessel now sails under the name of the *Far-Farer*, trawling not for herrings but for other catch. I explained all about the purpose of our journey during the drive from Ely, so we need not go through that again.

"The fearsome individual at the head of the

table is known as Major, because he's in the Army. He is no worse than he appears. Jon is on the top berth. He is next in age to you, an Icelander who speaks the language of Beowulf. What? You've never heard of Beowulf? No matter, few have.

"The giant by the door of the galley is Eric or Little by Little. He is our cook, learning cooking little by little, and he has just invented a pink pudding. They had it for dinner, that's why Doc is busy mixing up pills. You see, Cherry-Garrard was not at hand to try the pink pudding out on. Cherry, by the way, was born in the Antarctic, given to me as a pup, and is going to live with Jon's family when he returns to Iceland, Oxford being no place for huskies.

"The engine man is Fred, once a jockey at New-market, so likely to be useful with ponies. Handy-Andy is Andrew, the handy-man, financier of the cruise, coxswain of the *Far-Farer*, First Mate, purser, cabin boy, scullion, Jack of all trades and master of all too, steady as you go, hard a'port, etc. . . ."

The gigantic Eric dumped an enormous tea-pot on the table and interrupted the introductions.

"We'll all have tea if you've finished your non-sense, Jim. Fried steaks today, lads, all ready in my galley." He clattered out big mugs and tin plates. The Rev. Robert said Grace and they began the meal.

"I thought this was going to be a cruise for schoolboys," said Peter. "But I'm the only one."

"Cheer up, Jon's only sixteen. He has been staying with some friends in Oxford, that's how I came across him. I'm only nineteen myself. It's my beard that makes me look so aged. Have some bread and butter."

There were dozens of questions Peter wanted to ask, but hunger overcame curiosity. The ship's company sat on the lower berths, their legs tucked under the big table, which apparently had to do duty as a bed at night, berths and hammocks providing bedspace for only six at a time. A swinging lamp shed yellow light over the group, and the noise of their talking was deafening in so small a room. However, the steaks were smashing, eaten with chipped potatoes and dollops of tomato sauce, and hunks of crusty bread and butter, and swilled down with strong sweet tea, drunk from a walloping big mug, tasting quite different from the milky stuff one drank at home.

Perhaps Peter was tired after a day's journey, or exhausted by the heat of the cabin, or merely comfortable after a big meal, but his head began to droop as he sat, tightly wedged between Jewish David and Welsh Taffy, and soon he was sound asleep. He woke up at the sound of a great voice booming:

"Why, the kid's asleep. Is it his bedtime, Jim?"

Peter jerked himself awake. "I'm not asleep. I never go to bed as early as this. I want to see the boat."

"Come along with me," said the Rev. Robert.

"This cabin is mighty stuffy, and you'll be better in the open air. Up this way."

On deck the smell of salt was strong and fishier than ever. All around the *Far-Farer* lay other trawlers with red sails and squat funnels. There were yachts too, white-sailed and elegant, with here and there a shabby little cargo boat. All of them swayed slightly, rocking gently in their moorings by the quayside. The shades of evening drew in over the sea and lights went up at the harbour entrance. Beyond, Peter could see the grey tossing line of sea waters. He turned and looked towards the town, gaily lighted and still busy, with traffic roaring over the swing bridge.

"I suppose the bridge moves round to let shipping go up to Oulton Broad?" he said. "Is it far from here?"

"Not very far. I'm not sure of the exact distance. I believe Oulton Broad is a good centre for sailing and for fishing too. You called yourself Peter just now. Did you think of the Peter who was the fisherman whom Jesus called? 'I will make you fishers of men.' I wonder if Jesus is going to call you to follow Him too."

Peter did not reply. A dockside curate is a clergyman, and clergymen are expected to talk like that. No answer is required.

"I expect Jim James told you why we are spending our month's holiday in this way?"

"I didn't listen to his explanations. He talks too much."

Robert smiled. " Jim's tongue does wag a lot, but he's a splendid chap. We are going for this trip because we all, every one of us, love and serve the Lord Jesus Christ, and we want to help others to find Him as Saviour and Friend. That's why Jim undertook to bring you with him. We are going to start our campaign tonight. See, the skipper is putting up a big lamp on the mast and Jim is getting out his squeeze-box."

Peter sat down on a big coil of rope in the prow and watched while the far-farers collected on deck. The lamplight shone on Jim's yellow beard and his accordion. Beside him the Major stood stiff as a ramrod, glaring as if about to yell the order, " Charge! " The husky came and joined Peter on the rope. Jon and Fred perched on the railings near by. Peter wondered what an Icelander and a Newmarket jockey could be doing on a cruise. Surely there was no need for horses on the Broads. The *Far-Farer* was not a canal barge, and if she were, her horse would not be a racing animal.

> " Eternal Father, strong to save,
>   Whose arm hath bound the restless wave. . . ."

They all broke into song together, Jim James swung to and fro with his accordion. In the street, passers-by stopped to listen. Men came out of a public house, their beer glasses in their hands; heads popped up in other boats near by. The people in the Southwold bus passing over the bridge looked out with interest.

" Will your anchor hold in the storms of life?
    When the clouds unfold their wings of strife;
    When the strong tides lift and the cables strain,
    Will your anchor drift or firm remain? "

Over the darkening waters swept the answer:

" We have an anchor that keeps the soul
    Steadfast and sure while the billows roll;
    Fastened to the rock which cannot move,
    Grounded firm and deep in the Saviour's love."

Peter put his arm round Cherry-Garrard and leaned against the dog's furry coat. He was not at all sure what all this meant, but he enjoyed hearing the singing. Taffy had a glorious voice, and when he sang with David, you could see the crowd listening spellbound.

" Oh, the deep, deep love of Jesus!
    Vast, unmeasured, boundless, free;
    Rolling as a mighty ocean
    In its fulness over me."

Sung to the Welsh tune "Ebenezer" the hymn seemed just right, with the sea tossing out there beyond the harbour bar, and night falling over the port. The words rang out clearly without accompaniment, and in the silence which followed Robert stood forward to speak. He did not talk of the campaign he had mentioned to Peter, nor of his work in his dockside parish. He spoke only of Jesus, the Son of God, who came to this earth to seek and to save those who were lost.

"Criminals, murderers," thought Peter. "Wicked people are lost. Those are the ones who need to be preached to, like that surly brute standing on the jetty, or the cross woman beside him. I'm all right, of course. I've been properly brought up and educated, and I always try to play the game. I do the best I can, so this preaching isn't meant for me."

It was a comfortable thought, but he could not help wishing that Robert had not told the story of a boy who ran away from home and died alone in the backwoods, unable to save himself, unwilling to return although he had a loving and sorrowing father waiting for his son. "That's not in the least like me, I'm not lost," he thought.

"God made us for Himself. Without Him we are bound to be eternally alone, lost for ever. Jesus Christ came to this earth to seek and to save those who are like that. If you are far from God, wandering alone through life, then you are the very one for whom Jesus Christ is seeking tonight."

Once again David and Taffy sang together the second verse of the well-known hymn:

> "Oh, the deep, deep love of Jesus!
>   Spread His praise from shore to shore;
> How He loveth, ever loveth,
>   Changeth never, nevermore;
> How He watcheth o'er His loved ones,
>   Died to call them all His own;
> How for them He intercedeth,
>   Watcheth o'er them from the throne."

They moved about among the people on the quayside, talking with one and another, and Peter sat on his coil of rope watching them.

"They are not fishermen, though they look as if they were. They must be some sort of missionaries, I think, like the twelve Apostles. But there are only eleven, unless I'm counted as one too. Queer lot of apostles, an undergraduate and a doctor and a soldier and a miner. . . . I wonder what David does for a living, and Eric and Jon. . . . Funny Uncle Bill didn't say anything about them being religious, but that may have been in the letter Mavis tore up. They certainly are not the crowd of schoolboys Dad talked of. Poor old Dad, he was all het up with excitement and he didn't take in what the letter said before Mavis got hold of it."

"Give us another song, mates," bawled a rust-jerkined fisherman from another trawler. "Let's hear what the others of you have got to say."

So each of the eleven stood forward and spoke, some just a verse of Scripture, some a short message or story, and between the talks they sang with the onlookers joining in, and Peter too, when he knew the words. Beyond the harbour the sea thundered, but it was too dark now to see the grey waves. The ship's lantern made a circle of golden light above the heads of the eleven apostles, like a communal halo as they sang together their last song:

"O Christ, who in the wide world's ghostly sea
   Hast bid the net be cast anew, to Thee
      We sing our Alleluia.

To Thee, Eternal Spirit, Who again
Hast moved with life upon the slumbrous main,
    We sing our Alleluia.

Yea, west and east the companies go forth;
'We come' is sounding to the south and north;
    To God sing Alleluia.

The fishermen of Jesus, far away
Seek in new waters an immortal prey;
    To Christ sing Alleluia."

"I'm going to bed now," said Jon beside him in perfectly good English. "You will sleep in the top berth next to me. Come and I'll show you where it is. It is getting late."

He led the way back to the cabin and pointed to the pile of luggage stuffed beneath the lowest bunk.

"There's a case come for you by luggage in advance, but you'll hardly need it tonight. There's a lot of stuff on top."

Peter felt relieved. Uncle Bill must have sent his luggage on pretty quickly. Yes, he had things for the night in his bag. He undressed quickly and scrambled up into a fairly comfortable berth.

"If you are sea-sick, give me a shove and I'll call Doc."

"Me sea-sick! I've never been sea-sick in my life. Besides, it will be dead calm, the way we are going."

Peter always felt a bit superior with foreigners. Jon took no notice of his high and mighty ways.

"We shall be starting in the night. Aren't you going to say your prayers?"

"No fear. I'm too old for prayers." Peter cuddled down under the blankets, quite ready for sleep. Robert, Eric and David occupied the other berths and the table. Taffy swung a hammock across from one side to the other and curled up in it. Skipper May popped his frilly white head in for a moment and wished them good night.

"Just about ready, sir," he said to Robert. "It's a darty night."

A darty night at sea, but not up the river or on Oulton Broad. We'll have a smooth journey when the bridge swivels round and we move out of the harbour into the river. The water keeps clapping against the ship, making it rock. Peter shut his eyes firmly, determined to go to sleep.

Quietly the *Far-Farer* slipped from her mooring, but she did not sail riverwards. Out to the open sea she moved, and there she rocked and rolled and pitched and tossed, like a cork at the mercy of the waves.

"Are you all right, Ingolf?" called Jon, sitting up in his bunk.

"No, I'm not," came the muffled reply. "I think I'm going to die."

Chapter 3

ALL AT SEA

HE had never been sea-sick before, but that was because he had never been farther than a summer's day trip to the Isle of Wight and back. All his life he had enjoyed good health. He had never imagined that such suffering could be. At first the tossing made him afraid the boat would sink. Then he wished with all his heart that it would sink and quickly too, to put an end to his misery.

It was not only sea-sickness which alarmed him. When Jon went aloft to call Doc, he opened the cabin door and in rushed a blast of cold air, bringing the roar of the sea and the whistling of the wind. That made Peter Porter realize that the *Far-Farer* was making no quiet voyage along the Norfolk Broads. There were no schoolboys on this trip, no schoolmasters either. Sick as he felt, Peter sat up in bed and yelled at the top of his voice:

"Where are we going? Take me back. I'm on the wrong boat."

The other sleepers woke up and peered at him, astonished at the noise. He shouted again:

"I tell you it's a mistake. I ought to be going to the Broads. Where are you taking me to?"

Their oilskins dripping with rain and spray, Doc and Jim James clattered down the companion-way and crashed into the cabin.

"Cheer up, old man. You are not dead yet. Everyone has to have a dose of this before getting his sea-legs. You'll be O.K. tomorrow."

"Relax! Lie down and let yourself swing with the boat. Don't stiffen. Pretend you are floating on the water or swinging in a ham-mock. . . ."

Good advice was no great help. The horror of sea-sickness was infinitely increased by finding him-self completely at sea.

"You told me you were taking a party of school-boys on the Broads, Jim, but we are out in the open sea instead. Where are we going?"

"We are making for Iceland, as you very well know. I wrote and told Uncle Wilfred about our Evangelistic campaign, and he suggested we should take you with us. Don't make a fuss, Cyril; the sea is a bit rough tonight, but noth-ing to worry about. The skipper knows his way!"

"My name is not Cyril, and I haven't got an Uncle Wilfred. My uncle is William, Bill for short. You've made a ghastly mistake. I told you I was Peter Porter when we first met at Ely."

C

Jim James glanced at Doc, and Doc shrugged his shoulders. Jon climbed back into his bunk and the others lay back in theirs, prepared to sleep again.

"Listen, Cyril. We know that you are in the habit of playing practical jokes and that you vowed you would give trouble on this trip. We took the risk of that when we let you come. You have been spoilt by your fond mother and by Uncle Wilfred, your great-uncle, and they both admit it. They want you to find your feet and to toughen up a bit. That's why they let you join a crowd of men on a journey like this. Now no more nonsense. Go to sleep."

It was a wretched night. The waves buffeted the drifter and she rocked and heaved and lurched, the spray crashing on the deck. Up above, Peter could hear the duty crew shout from time to time, and occasionally there were sounds of singing. Doc came down and had a look at his patient once or twice, joking about *mal de mer* but offering no remedy beyond a constant reminder to relax and swing with the tide. Peter felt much too ill to bother about the relations of Jim James, and he did not care where the *Far-Farer* was going so long as she got there soon.

The storm died down by morning and it began to rain, a downpour which thundered on the deck above all day long. With an aching head and lurching insides Peter remained in his bunk, hating these so-called fishermen who were all so

tough that they did not show a single sign of
sickness. The smell of meals cooking in the
galley was loathesome. The sound of their singing and their bursts of laughter revolted him.
He was furious when any of them offered sym-
pathy.

The next morning Major came into the cabin
and hauled him out of bed.

"You young sluggard! You can't lie abed all
day and every day. Get up and go on deck. That's
the only way to cure sea-sickness."

Major listened to no arguments, and accepted
no symptoms as sufficient cause for convalescence.
He handed Peter his clothes and ordered him to
get dressed in a tone which brooked no dis-
obedience. Then he pulled a large suitcase out
from the stack of luggage and opened it.

"Your case came the day we sailed. Jim gave
me the key. Now, what have you got that's warm?
Put that on."

The large case was addressed to Cyril Copeland,
and its contents were evidently meant for a boy
of Peter's size. "That" was a woollen sweater
of extra thickness and abominable scratchiness,
but with Major's fierce eyes upon him Peter's
objections died away and he struggled into it.
Then, still feeling giddy and as if he were swimming into outer space, Peter followed Major on
deck.

The sea laughed a green glass mockery, glinting
in brilliant sunshine, with tossing white wave-

crests, and hollows of deepest blue. The wind cut his cheeks and brought back colour to his pale face, stirring the blood in his veins. The *Far-Farer* rose lightly on the green mountains and dipped into the blue hollows, slapping into the waves and riding triumphantly over translucent slopes. Peter gasped for breath, gulping in the keen air and suddenly felt a wild exhilaration. He was alive, well again, gloriously healthy. The feeble crock who had sobbed in the stuffy cabin was gone for ever.

"You are all right now," said Major. "Sit down on the lee side till you've got your legs. It's the fresh air you needed, not a lot of psychological treatment. And there is something else you need as well. That is a bit of plain speaking. You may as well drop all the lies and make-believe while you are with us. You are not Peter Porter. You are Cyril Copeland, and here is your passport to prove it."

He opened a slim dark blue book with a gold crest on the cover and there before him was the photograph of a boy. He had a flat sort of face, not unlike Peter's, but also not unlike ninety-nine boys out of a hundred, for it was not a very good photograph, and the expression was the wooden look usually put on by boys who do not wish to have their picture taken. The description of the holder of the photograph suited Peter too, for Cyril Copeland was the same age, within a few months, almost as tall, and had the same brown hair and grey eyes.

Neither had any special peculiarities, and both came from Nottinghamshire.

"I haven't told any lies," said Peter. "I am not Cyril Copeland. My name is Peter Porter, and my father told me to meet a man with a beard at Ely, a schoolmaster who is taking some boys on a cruise on the Broads. Jim James has a beard, and he said he was the man. He never mentioned Iceland . . ."

His voice trailed off suspiciously, for he remembered that Iceland had figured once or twice in the conversation, and there had been the half-hour harangue to which he had not listened at all.

"Stop playing the fool. We know all about you. Jim's uncle, your great-uncle, told him how you are continually pretending to be someone else. Your mother thinks it is the result of a lively imagination. Young Doc says it may be a mental state known as split-mind. Your uncle, and I heartily agree with him, knows that it is just a love of mischief for which you are now too old. A good spanking would have made you see reason long ago, and you'll get one if you play any games with me."

If Peter could have got hold of the unknown Cyril Copeland at that moment, he would have administered a good deal more than a spanking for getting him into this mix-up. But caution must be taken with the stern Major. He must play for safety. The other far-farers were inoffensive enough, being inclined to be sorry for a poor sea-sick lad far from home and mother. But not this guy! He backed away from Major and staggered round the deck, trying to keep his balance, and looking with interest at the engine-room and wheel-house.

A sheltered nook by the bridge made a sunny place to sit down and think things out. On the whole his adventure might have been worse. He had hit on a perfectly respectable crowd, not a gang of pirates or murderers. They were going to Iceland for a short time, so presumably they would bring him back again when they returned. He would see that they did not try to make him work as a cabin-boy for he was not going to be anybody's skivvy for nothing, but he would be sure to get some fun out of the voyage. Not every chap could have the opportunity of a journey to Iceland on a fishing trawler, even if the fishing was not of the usual sort. He did not remember much about Iceland, but he gathered it was quite civilized, so there would be a British Consul hanging round somewhere.

Yes, he would write a letter to Uncle Bill and explain what had happened. This he could post on landing, wherever they did land. Then he would make for the British Consul and tell his story, provided he could get away from this crowd of well-intentioned Christians.

"I feel like a lion that has got into a den of Daniels," he muttered. "If I behave awfully well

I may get caught by their religion. If I don't they'll eat me. . . . That reminds me, what's for dinner? "

He stretched his legs and found he could walk easier now. No use mucking round nursing a grievance. If they wanted to think he was Cyril Copeland, let them think it! They'd find out in the end that he wasn't, but in the meanwhile he might as well find out what was in Cyril Copeland's suitcase.

Cyril's clothes would fit him all right, he found, and Cyril's camera, with three colour films, was just the thing! He could get some good pictures with that. Cyril's adoring mother had tucked into every available corner some little delicacy, sweets, oranges, a cake, a tin of peaches, another of raspberries, a compass in case he lost his way, a writing-pad with envelopes. Where the real Cyril was, Peter had no idea. But if he had gone for the Broads cruise, he was not likely to have half such a good time as Peter Porter on his way to Iceland.

T.V. reports often mentioned depressions coming from Iceland, but there was no depression now, with the sunlight dancing over the swinging waters and the delightful smell of boiled salt beef with carrots, onions and parsnips coming from the galley. Dinner would not be ready just yet though, so what about visiting the wheel-house to help Skipper May steer his ship?

A coastal freighter came up over the horizon and

on the *Far-Farer* a bell rang. Up came Eric from his cooking, out came Major from the wireless cabin, and all the others from every direction. As the steamer approached, the far-farers hung out a huge banner over the side, scarlet with white letters:

JESUS SAVES

All together they broke into song:

"We have heard the joyful sound
 Jesus saves! Jesus saves!
Tell the message all around
 Jesus saves! Jesus saves!
Bear the news to every land
Climb the steeps and cross the waves.
Onward, 'tis our Lord's command;
 Jesus saves! Jesus saves!"

The crew of the freighter leaned over her side, staring at the banner and at the singers, waving a cheery greeting as their ship went its way. Peter returned to the ship's wheel and tried once more to steer a straight course. They passed quite a number of other craft, drifters and lighters, tugs and coasters, fishing boats, yachts and cargo boats of various nationalities. Every time the *Far-Farer* came near any ship out came the red banner and up raised the voices in song. It was not always the same hymn, and some Peter had sung at school prayers and could join.

In the afternoon they held a Bible-reading in a

sunny corner of the deck. Peter thought he had
better find out what they were doing, so he borrowed Cyril Copeland's Bible from the suitcase
and squeezed in beside Jim James and the dog.
It's something to do, he told himself. It will be
days before we get to Iceland.

Chapter 4

LAND AHEAD!

"LAND ahead! " called Skipper May from his bridge.

"Land ahead! " shouted Jim James down the hatchway to the chaps in the cabin.

"Land ahead! " yelled Peter Porter, waving Cyril Copeland's sou'wester at the smudge of grey-blue appearing on the far horizon. An off-shore wind blew spray into his face, stinging his tanned cheeks. A hardened seaman was Peter after five days in northern waters, as tough as any on board.

He was mighty glad to see dry land all the same. One gets bored with watching endlessly moving water and swooping sea-birds, and clouds racing. There had been plenty to do in galley, engine-room and wheel-house, games to play with Jim, Icelandic to learn from Jon and astronomy from David, who knew all about stars and planets and all that. There had been the Bible studies and discussions, and hymn-singings which he quite enjoyed, but all the same he was eager to go ashore and see what Iceland was like. And he wanted to prove to the others that he had not

lied when he said he was Peter Porter. He had
written long letters to his parents and to Uncle
Bill, explaining what had happened. Now at
last he would be able to post them and cable
to Dad's friend at R.A.F. Fenpool. Squadron
Leader Frost would be sure to be able to get on
an aircraft flying to Iceland and fetch Peter back
if need be.

He had failed entirely to convince the far-farers
that they were mistaken in believing him to be
the spoilt second cousin of Jim James. He had
boobed, he knew, by making an enemy of Major
from the very first. If he had cautiously offered
signs of friendship, Major might have been persuaded to transmit a message home by the ship's
wireless. But instead Peter had tried to do it
himself, and had put the whole set so completely
out of order that no further messages could be
sent or received for the rest of the voyage. Major
being the wireless expert, he had not unnaturally
showed signs of suspicion where Peter Porter was
concerned.

The misadventure with the wireless had caused
the other far-farers to mistrust his most innocent
remarks. He could not mention his family, for
they thought he was making up fairy tales. Talk
about the R.A.F. was taboo, for Cyril's late father
had been a pacifist, and had never been in any of
the Services. Still, on the whole they were a
decent crowd.

"We shall land at Reykjavik tomorrow," said

Jim James, coming to his side by the railing. "Then we leave the *Far-Farer* in dock with Skipper to take charge, and we all go off in parties so as to cover as much of the country as we can in the few days we have here. Taffy and David are the Western Party with Skipper, making their headquarters on board the *Far-Farer*. They will hold meetings in Reykjavik and the places round about, Hafnarfjördur and Keflavik and the west coast. Fred and Doc will disembark at Höfn, not far from here. They will be the Eastern Party, taking horses at Höfn and travelling eastwards from there. Fred is used to horses, though I cannot imagine what he will think of Icelandic ones. They cannot talk Icelandic, but they can distribute literature, and anyway many of the people can speak English. Jon's home is on the south coast, so his party will work from there. Handy-Andy and Eric and Jon will make a good team. The rest of us will be the Northern Party, and that includes you. We shall ride across country on horseback most of the way. Jon's father has very kindly made out an itinerary, marking our stopping places on a map, for we shall go to lonely isolated farms known to him, where Christian people will collect their neighbours for our meetings."

"We aren't stopping in Reykjavik then?"

"No. We shall go straight to Akureyri by bus. That is the most northerly town, and we can work from there."

"I'd rather stay with Jon. I don't like Major."

"You'll come with me, my dear coz. No running away, mind you. Iceland is no country to explore on your own, and I don't fancy chasing you through a land with no railways and precious few roads. You would soon come to a sad end among volcanoes, glaciers, hot springs, *geysirs* and deserts."

"I'd like to stay in Reykjavik with Skipper and Taffy and David."

"Why?" Jim James surveyed him with mistrust. "You will come with the Northern Party, and that reminds me, how much pocket-money have you got?"

"Five pounds."

Jim whistled. "Far too much for a kid like you. Hand it over. I shall take charge of it for you. Ask me for some when you want to buy anything and I'll give you enough."

The quarrel over the money was short and sharp. Jim James won, but not before Peter had accused him of thieving and kidnapping and many other crimes. Major intervened and took charge of the money himself, sealing it in an envelope, marked with the name of Cyril Copeland, which was infuriating, because if the real Cyril turned up he might claim the envelope and its contents. Hot, indignant and revengeful, Peter took refuge in the ship's lifeboat, planning revenge.

"Call themselves Christians, do they? Wicked thieves they are. I'll spoil their beastly Northern Party, see if I don't. Jim James is as bad as Major, every bit, him and his ridiculous yellow beard and his squawking accordion."

The accordion gave him the idea for part of his revenge. At least he could begin by putting a stop to the music on the trip. Major was much too reserved to sing unaccompanied. Jim and Robert could not do much on their own. To destroy the accordion was an easy way to pay out a thief and a bully. "Music reaches people's hearts," Taffy once said. The music of the old squeeze-box would never reach any but the cold hearts of fishes or the green hearts of mermaids.

He hopped out of the lifeboat, seized the accordion, which was lying on the raft, by the rust-red sail.

"Over she goes!" Out of the clear air, splash into the glassy waters bounced the treasure of Jim James. It floated pathetically, as if trying to get back and continue its part in the tour.

There was an angry shout from the bridge. Skipper May leaned out, his white whiskers bristling like a frill round his rosy face, and the gold of his East Anglian ear-rings glittering in the sunshine.

"Hey there! What yar up to?"

A second splash, louder than the first, was followed by a yell:

" Man overboard! "

From all directions, blue-guernseyed far-farers appeared in the twinkling of an eye, getting out the boat, for there was a nasty swell, and treacherous currents about. Peter stood watching a yellow head and beard bobbing about in the water, Jim James swimming to rescue his beloved accordion. He waited until the dripping owner of the dripping musical instrument was climbing up the rope ladder, and then cleared out of the way. It was impossible to hide in so small a ship, but the noise of the engine-room would safeguard him from any scolding.

He did not even get the satisfaction of seeing the annoyance of the company, for they said not one word to him about the matter and they were just the same as usual towards him when he appeared at mealtimes. Jim shut himself up with Handy-Andy in the little wireless room, where, presumably, they took the accordion to pieces and put it together again, but they did not mention what they were doing. Jim was a bit quiet that day, and looked bothered. Cherry-Garrard kept close beside his master, poking his cold nose into Jim's hand, and sitting outside the wireless room door while repairs were going on.

" He deserved what he got," said Peter.

The incident made one change. Robert came along to see the queer flat-topped mountains of the coastline and stood beside Peter for a while.

"You will be able to buy whatever you wish with your pocket-money," he said. "Major is keeping it, since you accused Jim of theft. But you have only to ask when you want to do any shopping."

"Jim had no right to take my money. He deserved to lose his beastly box of tricks."

"Jim's mother gave him that accordion. She is a widow with four children. It costs a good deal to send a son to Oxford, even if scholarships pay most of the fees, but Mrs. James has worked hard to enable him to have a good education. She knew he wanted an accordion and could not afford it, so she took a job cooking dinners at night for an hotel in order to buy one as a surprise for him. That accordion cost much more than money, Ingolf. It was Mrs. James' part in our adventure for Christ."

Peter's conscience began to make him feel uncomfortable, but he kept his chin up in the air.

"Jim James ought to have made sure that I was his cousin. I am no relation of his, and without my money I cannot prove it."

"I have discussed the matter with Jim and Major. We have decided to give up the first day of our tour and stay in Reykjavik. First thing in the morning we shall cable to Jim's uncle to find out what has happened to Cyril. Will that satisfy you?"

"No, it won't. You'll have to cable to my uncle

as well. Uncle Bill will have found out by now that I'm not on the Broads cruise."

Robert looked Peter straight in the eyes. "Yes, fair enough. We must cable to both uncles and wait for their replies. We shall not keep you with us if we find that you are the wrong boy. Handy-Andy, the chap who always lends a hand, has offered to pay for you to fly back from Keflavik airport, if it turns out that you are Peter Porter after all. Handy-Andy, as you have probably gathered, is already bearing most of the cost of this expedition, though we all pay part. Write down your uncle's address and that of the friend you mentioned in the R.A.F. Tomorrow morning you will see the sights of Reykjavik with Major, while Jim and I investigate."

"I'd rather come with you."

But Robert was not to be persuaded. Major would accompany Peter and that was that. Peter reflected gloomily that he had "had his chips". By revenging himself upon Jim James, he had caused a gulf to break between them. In future Jim would be polite, even pleasant, but he would never treat him again as a cousin, chattering away in that way he had, practising conjuring tricks, ventriloquism, sailors' knots, Icelandic conversation. The day after tomorrow Uncle Bill would cable to identify Peter Porter as his nephew, and Ingolf-cum-Cyril Copeland would vanish for ever.

D

The last day on board was full of excitements. The *Far-Farer* came close to the shore at the entrance to a fjord, behind which rose white mountains, the rim of the largest ice-cap in Europe, Vatnajökull, mysterious beneath a covering of fog. In answer to signals on the ship's siren a motor-boat came out of the fjord and into it stepped the Eastern Party, chubby casual Doc and Fred, who looked after the ship's engines, but who once had been a jockey at Newmarket. A strangely assorted couple, neither speaking a word of Icelandic, they hauled down huge packs of literature from the Bible Society and the motor-boat buzzed off, to the sound of singing from the *Far-Farer*, and watched by the inhabitants of the little town of Höfn, just inside the fjord.

Then on, skirting the coast until they came to another fjord, and another motor-boat, in which this time there sat a grey-haired man and two girls, Jon's father and sisters come to meet him. Helga, the elder one, was a laughing, golden-haired girl, and the younger, Solvieg, was gentle and rather shy. They waved and smiled at Peter as he stood watching from the deck. Handy-Andy, Eric and Jon took their baggage and climbed down the ladder into the swaying boat, and off it went.

> "Speed Thy servants, Saviour speed them
>   Thou art Lord of winds and waves;
>   They were bound, but Thou hast freed them,

Now they go to free the slaves.
 Be Thou with them,
'Tis Thine arm alone that saves."

The Southern Party had set out on their journey.
The adventure for Christ had begun.

Chapter 5

SMOKY BAY

THEY sailed past the desolate Westmann Islands and round the rugged coastline to the wide bay of Faxa Flói. Sixty miles away on the far side of the bay they could see the outline of a great mountain, shining white in the morning sun.

"That's Snaefelljökull, the glacier with a volcano underneath," cried Taffy. "Did you ever see anything so grand, man? This is a fine country indeed, an island of frost and fire, snow above and boiling water beneath. Jon told me Reykjavik is heated from hot springs, so that when you turn on your tap, boiling water always comes out. You have to fill your bath early and let it cool enough for you to get in. Man, it is indeed an interesting place we have come to. No need for electricity or coal, but hot water laid on for nothing. Smoky Bay, they call it, because of the steam from the hot springs."

The wild lonely shores they had passed had made Peter expect to find Reykjavik a dreary little shack town with a rough jetty. But, standing on deck as they approached, he saw a wide harbour, protected by a long breakwater, and quays where lay plenty of other shipping. There were cranes for loading and unloading, a big coal grab, and even a railway line.

"That's Iceland's only railway," laughed Taffy. "Fifty yards of track for transportation in the docks. Mind you don't get knocked down by Iceland's only train, Ingolf."

Along the waterfront Peter could see warehouses, offices and shops. Behind, houses were built on the hillside, rising up from the harbour, modern, clean houses with the sun shining on startlingly coloured roofs, red-tiled or blue-slated, tin roofs painted green or a coppery brown. Those roofs gave one the impression that it was a toy town, so fresh and new and quaint.

Seagulls swooped over the shipping, as they tied alongside a stone pier. There was already a big passenger ship not far away, *M.S. Gullfoss* painted on her side.

"Gullfoss means 'Golden Fall'," said Peter, not to be outdone by Taffy's show of knowledge. "Jon says there are lots of waterfalls in Iceland, Gullfoss and Godafoss and Dettifoss, and lots more."

"Godafoss means 'the Fall of the Gods'. It is the place where the Icelanders threw away their Gods, when they became Christians long ago."

"I don't know why you came here to preach to heathen. They are Christians, quite as civilized as we are. Look, they have buses and cars and shops and houses. They even drive on the left side of the road as we do. It isn't as if they were Eskimos, living in igloos, or blacks worshipping witch doctors."

"Icelanders and British, Eskimos and Africans, we all need a Saviour, for we are all sinners. Snaefelljökull looks clean enough when you see him in the distance, gleaming whiter than white indeed. But he has got fire in his heart."

"I'm not a sinner, nor is my father nor my mother. We don't go to church or read the Bible."

"If you had read the Bible you would have seen that it says that we are all sinners, and so we are and no mistake. It's a coal miner I am, Ingolf, and well I know that coal is black, even if you whitewash it over the top. No disrespect to your parents, lad, but every one of us needs to be changed inside, our hearts washed whiter than snow."

"Well, why pick on Iceland?"

"Because us chaps were all burning to do a bit of missionary work, and yet we were all in jobs or in training for jobs. We had our holidays to spend as we chose, and this is the way we took. The time on board has been grand, a little convention for us, prayer and Bible study and rejoicing together. Now for a week of spreading the good news to people who can't often go to church or have any opportunity of hearing the Gospel. We are all young and strong. Good sailors we are, and we'll enjoy riding over wild trackless country, singing the songs of Zion and preaching, those of us that know the lingo well enough. Man, it's a grand life."

Taffy's eager, dark eyes, his untidy black hair blowing in the wind, and his Welsh voice trilling out his ardent faith, made Peter feel rather cold and empty, as if he had missed something. He returned to his survey of what he could see of the town.

After breakfast he was to see Reykjavik more thoroughly, but not inspired this time by Taffy's Celtic enthusiasm. Major was to be his escort, the man whom he had most avoided all through the voyage. Regretfully he watched David and Taffy ride off in a car, driven by a Jewish relation of David's, an old gentleman who had taken refuge in Iceland many years earlier, fleeing from persecution in Europe. Now a Christian Jew, he was willing to throw in his lot with those who came to preach the Gospel in the land of his exile.

Peter walked a little behind Major, in order to avoid conversation, listening unwillingly when Major pointed out items of interest.

On a rocky plateau, overlooking the city and harbour, the statue of a sturdy Viking standing on the prow of a ship called forth the information that it represented Leif Eriksson, the man who discovered America.

"It was Christopher Columbus who discovered America. Everyone knows that," objected Peter.

"They both discovered America. Leif Eriksson

won the race by five hundred years, but he was not known so well as Columbus. He was only a hero in his own isolated little country, whereas Columbus sailed to America at a time when Spain was great and powerful, so news of his discovery inspired the whole world. They both discovered a new world."

"You need not start preaching at me. I know I'm right. Is that the church where the Western Party are going to have their children's service this afternoon?"

"Not that one; a church by a lake. They are going to borrow Jim James, since we cannot start our journey today. Jim is splendid at preaching to children. Not everyone is gifted that way."

Peter smiled sourly. He had heard the plans for the afternoon and did not think much of them. Jim James had learned one sermon off by heart in Icelandic. It was a sermon he had heard in England, and he had got Jon to translate it for him, and that sermon was to be produced whenever Jim got a chance of preaching. It seemed a pretty poor plan, although to be sure learning that one sermon by heart had been a stupendous task for Jim, who did not know much Icelandic.

There were dozens of bookshops in Reykjavik, and there were shops where you could buy delicious things to eat; shops which sold pictures of Icelandic scenery and postcards; shops where you saw sealskin goods, and models of Icelandic birds, puffins, ravens, terns and pink-foot geese.

But Peter was too proud to ask for his pocket-money, and the Major marched on, as if leading a company of soldiers on manœuvre. They saw a square with flowers and small trees, where there was a cathedral and the Parliament building and a big hotel. They went round the museum and the National Library and presently they came to another statue of a Viking on the dragon-prow of a ship.

"Leif Eriksson again, I suppose," growled Peter.

"No, your namesake this time. Ingolf, the first Norse settler. He took to Iceland, rather better than you seem to have though, and decided to live here. There's a story about him. . . ."

"I don't want to hear it. What about having some elevenses? I'm hungry."

They found a place called the Garden Café, on account of its glass-roofed sun-trap, which was adorned with pots of flowers and ferns. Major ordered coffee for himself, and Peter chose an ice-cream covered with hot chocolate sauce, creamier and more chocolatey than anything he had ever imagined. The real Cyril Copeland must be a mug, he decided, to choose the Norfolk Broads and reject a place like this, where such delicacies were available. He wondered as he ate what had happened to Cyril. Had he gone home, saying he had missed his cousin Jim? Had he never left home at all? Or had he gone on the Broads cruise with the real man with a beard? What had Uncle Bill and Aunt Eva said when the bearded schoolmaster informed them that Peter Porter had not turned up? He had asked himself all these questions countless times in the last week. Now the answer to them all must be speeding on its way to Reykjavik. Robert and Jim James would tell him when he got back to the *Far-Farer* for dinner.

Around them Icelandic people chatted in their strange tongue and tourists of various nationalities in theirs. Suddenly Peter became aware that a very pretty girl of about nineteen was coming towards their table with a delightful smile as if she was surprised and glad to see them. He kicked Major under the table. Major stopped stirring his coffee in an absent-minded way and looked up.

"Why, Gerald!" cried the girl. "Fancy meeting you here in Iceland of all places! Whatever are you doing? You look just like a fisherman!"

Major sprang to his feet, his bronzed face flushing. Peter stood up too, not without a feeling of annoyance that he must put up with Major's friends as well as his horrible self.

"Daddy decided to come for a week's fishing, so Mummy and I flew over with him, just to see this strange island. Isn't it fascinating, all *geysirs* and volcanoes? Is this your little brother?"

"Little." That finished her in Peter's estimation. He did not think much of girls anyway, but a girl who was idiotic enough to call him little was beneath contempt. And he objected to the suggestion of a relationship with Major. It was bad enough to be thought a cousin of Jim James!

Then the girl's mother came over and her father, who turned out to be the colonel of Major's regiment. Peter put his foot in it with the military type by calling his companion "Major", for it appeared that he was only a Second Lieutenant. Major was just Jim James' nonsense, a nickname for a very young but efficient officer.

Uneasily, Peter shifted from one foot to the other, watching his perfect ice-cream dissolving into a mushy liquid beneath its coating of hot sauce. He hated social occasions and his only comfort was that Major did not appear to be enjoying the unexpected meeting either. He stood stiffly erect, courteous but unsmiling.

At last the colonel, the colonel's lady and the colonel's daughter took their departure, having failed to induce Major to accept an invitation to lunch at the Borg Hotel or to join them in an expedition to see the *geysirs* on the morrow.

" Is that the girl you are going to marry? " asked Peter, by way of revenging himself for his lost ice-cream. One glare from Major sufficed for an answer, and decided Peter on his next course of action. There was no point in running away, since he must hear the result of the cablegrams sent to Uncle Bill and Jim's uncle, but he might as well have the rest of the morning to himself. While Major was paying the bill, Peter took to his heels.

Exploring Reykjavik by himself would be fun.

No need now to bother where he went or what he saw. He pelted up the hill, threading his way past the shoppers and turning off to the left and again to the right. A cautious glance behind him showed that Major was not following. Now he could take his time.

He turned down a pretty road leading to water. There was water everywhere in Reykjavik, at the bottom of every hill you saw it gleaming, the harbour, the bay, or the fjord. The houses on the hillside had gardens with flowers. At the foot of the hill there was a church with a neat bell tower on top. And the church lay beside a lake, shimmering in the sun.

"The church by the lake where Jim is going to preach his famous sermon," Peter laughed. "They'll all come down here this afternoon, all except Jim, who will have to escort me to Keflavik to see me off back to England by aeroplane."

He felt almost sorry that his stay in Iceland should be so short.

Chapter 6

EXILES

THERE was a park beyond the church, a pretty place with gay summer flowers and bushes of flowering shrubs. The trees were few and small; rowans white with blossom, and dainty birches. A bridge led the way to an island in the lake and a crowd of brightly coloured ducks were feeding by the water's edge. Tired with running, Peter sat down on the grass to watch them. Presently a man came along and sat down beside him.

"Foreign sort of ducks these," observed the man.

"English are you?" asked Peter.

"No business of yours what I am. I seen you just now with Mr. Lang."

So this seedy-looking individual knew Major, did he? What was he up to in Reykjavik?

"What's Mr. Lang dressed up like a fisherman for?"

"He's with a party of missionaries or something. They came here in a trawler from Lowestoft."

The man swore. "He would do that sort of

thing. A Christian, ain't he? I know him. Doesn't drink. Doesn't swear. Goes to church and breaks a girl's heart. That's his type."

"Did he break the colonel's daughter's heart?" asked Peter with interest.

"You know her, do you? So do I. Batman I was in the Officers' Mess. We know a thing or two, us batmen. All the young subalterns were in love with her, but she's got eyes for none but him, that won't give a glance her way. Cold fish, Mr. Lang, cruel, he is."

Peter was quite willing to believe the worst of Major, even though he did not think any too highly of the seedy-looking chap beside him.

"How long's he going to be in Iceland? What's he come for?"

"It isn't your business. I'm not telling you his plans."

The man had a hungry look about his thin face, almost as if he had had nothing to eat for days. His voice was sad and pathetic as he spoke:

"Say, kid, you might help a chap that's on the rocks. I only want to know whether Mr. Lang is after me or not, that's all. You see, I'm a deserter. Got into a row in the Army for bashing an officer on the head. He was a nasty type and deserved it. I didn't kill him, mind, but I got sentenced to twelve months in the glasshouse. Mr. Lang he came in when we was fighting, so he witnessed against me. He was so dead set on telling the truth, he wouldn't even pass a white one to save me. Ruined me, he did."

Peter knew quite well that Major would not have told lies at a court-martial or anywhere else. He began to feel sorry for the thin sad deserter.

"How did you get to Iceland?"

"I was on my way to Colchester under armed escort, but I gave them the slip. Hid up for a bit and then got a job on a cargo boat and landed up here. I had a row with one of the crew and cleared out. . . ."

"You quarrel a lot, don't you? What are you going to do now?"

"I want to get to the States, if I can. Help me, mister."

There was not much that Peter could do. He had no money to offer and he knew nothing of Major's reasons for joining the far-farers.

"He hasn't said anything to me about coming after you. As far as I know, he hasn't any idea you are here. But I'd advise you to get away quickly, because the colonel of his regiment is in Reykjavik as well as Mr. Lang. We met him and his wife and his daughter in the Garden Café this morning."

The man groaned. "Have they sent him out too? They're after me and they'll get me in the end. Look, kid, don't tell on me. You won't squeal, will you? I'd help you if you was in need, I vow I would."

His face was so flushed and his eyes so bright, that Peter realized he was ill. Perhaps he was starving or had double pneumonia. Not knowing much about illness, Peter was unable to say what was the matter. A slab of fruit and nut chocolate, the last of Cyril's titbits packed by his loving mother, was all the refreshment he possessed. By the way the deserter grabbed it, starvation appeared to be what was wrong with him.

"I shouldn't worry about Major or his colonel. They wouldn't come all this way after a deserter. They'd send a couple of military police or else they'd just forget you. My Dad's in the R.A.F., so I know."

Just as suddenly as he had come, the man disappeared, vanishing behind the bushes, and streaking off towards the town. Peter saw why he had gone off so quickly. Major was swinging along the path searching for his charge. What a cruel bully he must be, to scare a weak, miserable creature like that deserter! Fancy coming all the way to Iceland to track down a half-starved weakling and to drag him back to England for weeks of weary punishment in prison! What a stern way he had of pressing his lips together, and how white and set his face was! All the same, it was dinner-time and the results of the cabled enquiries must be ready now. Peter went to meet his enemy with his chin in the air, determined to show how he despised the fellow.

Robert and Jim were in the wheel-house with Skipper, drinking strong tea and getting outside plates of fried ham.

"Hallo! What did Uncle Bill have to say about you kidnapping his nephew?" asked Peter jauntily.

Robert put down his cup and met Peter's eyes. Jim turned his back and looked seawards. Peter took the telegram form and read it:

"Peter enjoying cruise. Has written twice. Camp Commandant completely satisfied. Porter."

"But I haven't written . . . at least I haven't posted the letter because I hadn't any stamps."

"Jim's uncle is on the telephone. We were able to speak directly with him, though only for a short time, as the cost of telephoning is high. This is what he said: Cyril left home early without saying good-bye, but he left a note explaining that he intended to meet his second cousin Jim at Ely, and, as he did not wish to go on an Evangelistic tour, he was determined to give as much trouble as possible to all the farfarers."

Peter opened his mouth but no words came. He simply could not say all over again that he was not Cyril, and Cyril was not Peter. There was no convincing these chaps. Robert went on in his quiet way:

"Fetch a plate of dinner from the galley and stop pretending, Ingolf. We know your game now, and we both agree you have acted very well

E

the part you chose to play. I almost believed that you really were your friend Peter Porter. But the farce is over and we will not carry it on any longer."

Peter went below to find his dinner and as he went he considered the situation. So the real Cyril had had the cheek to take his place on the Broads cruise, had he? All right, let him enjoy the waterways of Norfolk with windmills and quiet level country. Cyril had got Peter's luggage in advance, a case full of all his oldest clothes, because Mother knew he would mess them up on the Broads. He'd got Peter's aged box camera, which had belonged to Dad as a boy, and Peter's holiday tasks too, set in advance by his form master. Cyril could have his holiday on the Broads if he wished, free, gratis, for nothing! It would be a fortnight shorter than the cruise of the far-farers! Peter would see Iceland, even if it did mean a good deal of church-going. He would have Cyril's splendid camera with flashlight apparatus and colour films too. He would have all Cyril's excellent clothes, his case of specimens, his press for flowers, his torch, everything, including the sweets already eaten.

They were talking about the children's service when he got back to the wheel-house. Two o'clock in the Lakeside Church, and they were all as thrilled about it as if they had been going to a Cup Final. Daft, it seemed to Peter, but he could not help becoming interested, what with Jim

James and his precious sermon, learned by heart in Icelandic, and Taffy's choice of hymns which he intended to teach the children.

They went in a bunch to the Lakeside Church after dinner, Skipper and Robert and Jim and Major and David and Taffy and the Jewish Icelandic hosts and the pastor of the Lakeside Church too. And the children poured in, for they had school holidays here in the long summer days. Pretty children they were, mostly fair-haired, and all well-dressed and healthy, as if they had been fed on cod-liver oil all their lives. "Fish-heads", Peter called them with a vast feeling of superiority, but he thought them a decent crowd and he liked the church too, all painted in dainty colours, pale blue and white with dark brown pews. It was light and airy, not dim and solemn like the churches he had visited with Jim on the way to Lowestoft.

Jim James was at his best with children, and so was Taffy. The eager little Welsh miner got that crowd singing with fervour, though they were not used to such lively tunes. When they were all quite exhausted with singing, Jim James started off on his famous sermon.

You could have heard a bat squeak, if there had been any bats there! The children listened spell-bound, gazing entranced at Jim's golden hair and beard and his sparkling blue eyes. Peter forgot his annoyance about the pocket-money and his anger with Cyril. He could only listen to those Icelandic words, learned so earnestly by heart, and now poured out so fluently. It was an illustrated sermon, so all the more easy to follow. Jim held up a big horse-shoe magnet, and took from his pocket a bag of nails, big nails, little nails, crooked nails, straight nails, broken nails, old nails, every kind of nail, and all could be picked up by the magnet. It was easy to get the meaning of that sermon, easy to see, even if, like Peter, one didn't want to understand it.

"I think I ought to get back to England, and go to Uncle Bill, for if I stay with this crowd, the Magnet may pick me up," thought Peter. "It's more catching than chickenpox."

Towards the end of the sermon, someone brought in a little note to the pastor, which he presently read aloud to the children. It was a message from a well-known preacher to children who was staying for a few days in Reykjavik. He had heard of the service and would like to say a few words to the children before they dispersed. Peter groaned. More sermons! He had got through Jim James' effort successfully, and surely that was enough. But the young Icelanders gasped with delight. They knew and loved the famous preacher and were only too willing to wait for more.

He came in, tall, stately and benevolent, with his black robe and little white tabs beneath his chin, quite different from Jim James.

Jim's face went rosy red where it could be seen

above his beard. His back stiffened. Peter wondered why. Then he saw.

The famous preacher drew out from his black pocket a large horse-shoe magnet and a bag of nails, big nails, little nails, crooked nails. . . .

The young Icelanders behaved with perfect courtesy and infinite tact. Peter Porter disgraced himself and his nation by breaking into a great guffaw of laughter. Major seized him by the ear and hauled him out of church.

He laughed and laughed and laughed, but Major's face was grim as usual.

"So that was the man who preached the sermon Jim James never forgot. He'll never forget it now if he lives to be a million, nor will I, nor you!"

"It is not an original sermon," explained Major. "Neither the famous preacher nor Jim made it up. The sermon on the magnet has been preached to children countless times. Some things are worth repeating. It was far better for Jim to start off with a simple message like that than to embark on a discourse above the heads of his congregation. That the sermon was repeated a second time is no reason for behaving badly in church."

Then he marched Peter round and round the lake until the second edition of the magnet sermon had come to an end and the children came pouring out of the church.

Taffy joined them, radiant, delighted.

"That was a powerful sermon of Jim's, was it not? Never have I been so moved, even though I cannot understand Icelandic. The children listened so well, and then to think that the message has been impressed upon their hearts, by being repeated all over again! It could not have happened better. All things work together for good to them that love God. Our Western campaign has begun well."

"And now we must start off on the Northern campaign," said Major. "Come on, Ingolf, back to the *Far-Farer*. We must collect our packs."

"What, tonight?"

"Right away. We are going to catch the bus to Thingvellir, a good starting-off place. Thingvellir is the seat of the old Icelandic Parliament."

"I'm sick of parliaments. We saw one this morning."

"You'll see another this evening. The place of the law may do you good." And as they walked back to the docks, Major discoursed about the origins of Iceland, the volcanic ridge lying under the sea from Greenland to Iceland, to the Faroes and on to Scotland. A young land, Iceland, one of the latest land masses to appear, built up entirely by layers of basalt, each layer representing a flood of lava, which poured out from some crack in the earth's surface.

It might have been rather a depressing walk if David had not joined them and talked of what he had heard of that same country. How beautiful it was in summer-time, with its few frail flowers and its graceful mosses and lichens. Snow-capped mountains, silver streams, green pasture lands, and the flashing glories of the Northern Lights all combined to make it one of the loveliest countries of the world.

"But there is one that is lovelier," said David. "Palestine, my homeland, which I have never seen. It is the desire of my heart to walk in the footsteps of my Saviour, to see the hills He saw, to sail on the lake where He sailed. That is the loveliest country on earth, and we are promised one even lovelier in Heaven."

"There is a colour film in Cyril's camera. I shall begin by taking photos of this Thingvellir, if it is worth taking. Then I'll send them to my parents in Singapore."

David and Major exchanged glances and smiled.

Chapter 7

THE PLACE OF THE LAW

THEY took the bus to Thingvellir, carrying
their luggage in rucksacks and bundles, and
wearing stout shoes for walking and raincoats,
for Thingvellir was to be the starting-place of the
travels of the Northern Party.

"Jim said we were going straight to Akureyri
by bus all the way," objected Peter.

"We have changed our plans," said Robert, but
he did not explain whether it was the information
received that morning or Peter's disturbance in
church which had caused the alteration. Peter
had an unpleasant feeling that Thingvellir was
one of those educative museum shows which the
far-farers felt their young companion ought not
to miss. He was fully prepared to detest the place
of the law for that reason.

Still, the journey was not too bad, in fact if
he hadn't felt that he was being improved he
would have enjoyed every moment. The other
passengers in the bus were interesting, a big
party of boys and girls all going to camp on the
historic site, and a group of elderly Icelandic
ladies in their national costume. For about thirty-

five miles they bounced along, seeing first the out-skirts of Reykjavik, the most astounding suburbs any city ever possessed, with their steamy springs and hot-houses filled with tropical fruit and flowers; the power-plant, the antennae of the long-wave broadcasting station, just as if Reykjavik was the most modern of towns; then tumbled, fantastic mountains and stretches of grey lava-strewn coun-try, pitted and scarred as if it had been scenery on the face of the moon. There were isolated farms, little fields, whose soil was so scarce and precious that it had to be fed with the decaying remains of fishes, a gruesome spectacle. Along the side of the road ran a covered aqueduct bring-ing hot water to the city, an excellent cycling track it would make, in Peter's estimation. On the mountainous part of the way, there were cairns built to guide travellers in winter . . . not that you would have thought that many people travelled that way except in summer, until you came to the ski club. That made Peter almost wish that the far-farers had chosen a winter cruise.

"What-ho, Ingolf! Behold an extinct volcano, a crater and yet another crater, and another one after that! " Jim James was beginning to recover his spirits. "Look on the left, Ingolf, an Arctic Tern. On your right, an Arctic Tern, turning and turning . . . nothing else to do, I suppose. Ahead, a plain of lava, behind a plain of lava . . . all around, a plain of lava. . . ."

Jim James' nonsense soon got the Icelanders into conversation, and then, hey presto! out came the damaged accordion, rather squeaky now and not quite so beautiful, but game to the end. In a trice the whole busful were singing until suddenly out of the plains they swept, down into a steep gorge, leading between walls of strange rock formation, leading to a wide green plain with a lake.

"Once this plain was a sea of boiling lava. Now it is the most famous spot in Iceland, and we are going to pitch our tent and sleep here tonight."

It was not in any way the sort of ruined ancient monument Peter had expected. Crowds of gay tents dotted the grass and campers swarmed about with cars and charabancs. Beside the water stood a neat yellow church, very small and tidy, with a parsonage house with three wide gables and a turfed roof. There was a big hotel and boats on the lake. Robert got tea ready and Major pitched the tent, while Jim and Peter rounded up the other campers to play cricket.

It was an odd cricket match, most of the players never having played the game before. The evening lasted so long that there was no need to draw stumps until everyone was too sleepy to go on with the game. Then they sat round the camp fire and sang again and Robert talked. It was not dark all night, only just a faint twilight came creeping over the scene and then faded away in the glory of the dawn. It was strange to sing an evening hymn like:

"The day Thou gavest, Lord, is ended,"

when no darkness came to cover the land. The second verse was more appropriate:

"As o'er each continent and island,
    The dawn leads on another day,
The voice of prayer is never silent,
    Nor dies the strain of praise away."

Peter got up early in the morning and went off to explore on his own, taking Cyril's camera to get some pictures. The first snap he took was of some Icelandic boys tramping together, like a gang of wandering Vikings, their fair hair blowing in the wind. They were pleased to be photographed and soon made friends, telling him in quite excellent English all about the olden days, when the Allthing, Iceland's parliament, was held at Thingvellir, and the great camping there was with sporting festivals, horse-fighting, racing and wrestling. They showed him "the Glima", their way of wrestling, and soon knocked him out, but it was good sport.

"Come, see the Bank of Iceland," they cried, and led him to a deep pool in whose gleaming depths he saw thousands of coins, dropped in by people who had passed that way. Peter felt in all Cyril's pockets, but not a krona nor an eyrir was there, not so much as a half-penny piece.

"Oxarafoss," called the boys and off they ran to see the waterfall, tumbling sunlit and laughing from the rocks.

"Hush! Here is the Drowning Pool!" They leaned over the steep sides of a gloomy tarn and whispered the dreadful story of the punishment for murderers and wicked people, dropped into the dark water in a weighted sack.

Then suddenly the Viking boys ran off together, whooping out some lilting song of their own, and Peter stood alone in the fresh morning air. He decided that it must be breakfast-time.

"What did you see on your ramble?" asked Jim, turning a rasher of bacon in the frying pan.

"I saw three waters, the pool for money and the pool for punishing wicked people and the waterfall with the sun in it."

"Three ways to die," said Robert. "There's the man who piles up money and worldly goods and must leave them all behind; the man who chooses the path of sin and goes to his punishment, and there is the man who opens his heart to the Light of Life and finds death the dawn of a new and better day."

"Well, I'm not any of those three. I haven't any worldly goods, because Major has stolen them. I'm not a sinner, and I'm not a Christian either."

"You must be one or the other. Listen: 'Thou

shalt love the Lord thy God with all thy heart
and with all thy soul and with all thy mind
and with all thy strength.' I do not think any
of us have done that, so we are all sinners."

Peter carved himself a big chunk of bread. He
did not wish to think about sin or the dark pool
of punishment.

After breakfast they divided the baggage between them, each taking a share, though Peter's
was considerably lighter than the other three
bundles. Ten miles there was to walk to the
farm where Jon's friends lived and where the
far-farers would be able to get ponies for the next
stage of their journey. They set out cheerfully,
tramping over the soft meadows and through the
undergrowth which was considered a forest in that
treeless land. They stopped to take photographs
of the reindeer which are found in the lonely
region at the far side of the lake, and then on
over a sandy desert place where few plants grew
and no birds sang.

Away in the mountains they found the farm,
and there a kindly old man welcomed them to a
delicious meal, prepared by his wife. Pancakes
they had, and sweet soup, coffee and an Icelandic
dish called *Skyr*, a mixture of sour cream and
sugar. Whether it was lunch or tea, they did not
know, but it tasted good. Peter left the others
to their conversation, and wandered out to see
the horses. He had never ridden anything more
lively than a seaside donkey, but these shaggy

creatures were more like ponies than horses, and they looked quiet and manageable. They were grazing on the rough grass by their turf-roofed stable, and he studied them with interest. There was a black mare, a dappled grey and a roan, and a delightful young chestnut with dark mane and tail. In the distance two piebalds were gambolling together.

"I'll choose the chestnut," said Peter.

But it was not to be. When the old man came out, he said firmly that only an experienced rider could manage "Snorri", for the chestnut was wild and barely broken in. His grandson, he declared, a boy of the same age as Peter, much preferred to ride the docile Grettir, dappled grey and elderly.

Major decided the question. Snorri should carry the baggage; Peter should ride Grettir, he and Jim the piebalds, and Robert the roan. It was like Major to cut in and order people around. What did he know of horses any more than the rest of them? He wasn't in the cavalry. There were no mounted regiments now.

Surly and resentful, Peter rode off on Grettir, a fat lump of pudding, this horse, quiet and demure, not a spark of life in him.

The sun was hot in the afternoon, riding along the sheltered pass among the mountains. The heat and the flies and the sand made Peter feel crosser than ever. He objected to the way Major rode first in the narrow path, taking the lead all the time, though Robert was really the head of the expedition.

Presently they came to a cottage where some children were playing. Peter wandered off to watch a woman washing sheepskins in a stream. They were thick black fleeces and they didn't get much cleaner for their laundering. He would have liked to ask why she washed them and what they would be used for, but the woman did not understand English. He looked round cautiously. Yes, just as he had expected, Jim James was getting out his accordion. He was going to teach the children a chorus, singing the Gospel message, his way of helping them to remember the Bible words. Robert was deep in conversation with the man of the house. Major was helping a youth to pile strips of brown turf on a cart. Nobody was looking his way.

He stepped quickly towards the horses, quietly cropping the grass. Snorri, the chestnut, was the gentlest of all, and the handsomest. He lifted the pack from his back and transferred it to that of the dappled-grey Grettir. Then up he sprang and away like the wind.

Snorri was a beauty. After the slow jogging of old Grettir, this was the real thing, cantering over the meadowland on sure-footed, clear-sighted Snorri, a king among ponies. But when the meadow grass came to an end, and Snorri found himself on marshy wet ground, he hesitated, tossing his thick mane uncertainly. He did not know which way to go, and Peter did not either, so Snorri made his own decision. Leaving the boggy ground, he headed straight for the river, a wide, sluggish, shallow stream, bordered with sedges, out from which scattered a crowd of startled water-fowl.

Snorri was accustomed to swimming across such rivers, but Peter could not know that. He tugged and pulled, but could not change direction. The pony waded out to midstream, which was half-way to the saddle, and then, evidently deciding that the water was not deep enough, the creature turned and went downstream. Peter let out a yell then which scared poor Snorri and he shied, snorting, kicking up his heels, splashing, with Peter clinging on to his mane, struggling to keep his seat.

There was a shout behind him, and the pony stood still. Major on his piebald had ridden into the water, seized Snorri's reins and was calming him, quietly leading him back to dry ground. Jim and Robert came running to the river's bank. All the Icelandic family stood staring, and Major assisted Peter to dismount with a face colder than all the glaciers in Iceland. He did not say a word, but put the baggage all on the second pack-horse, and let Snorri run without a load to calm him down. Peter, crestfallen, mounted Grettir once again, thankful at least that he had been spared a ducking.

"Here's a good place for tea," said Jim after

a long and silent ride. "Nothing like a cup of tea for cheering one's spirits. We can tether the horses to the fence here, so Ingolf won't go galloping off on his own."

The jest annoyed Peter. It was a lovely spot, but he took no pleasure in it. The meadow sloped down towards the river, and the boggy ground between the picnic site and the water was white with tufted cotton-grass. The bank where they sat was a gay carpet of flowers, dandelions, buttercups, pinky-white cuckoo-flowers, purple cranesbill and yellow potentilla. A brood of goslings scuttled away at their approach, and at the water's edge dainty little dunlins stepped elegantly in the slime. But neither birds nor flowers, nor the background of purple mountains, slashed by the green glacier could bring a smile to the face of Peter Porter.

"I hate the lot of you," he announced. "Sanctimonious, self-righteous prigs, that's what you are, singing hymns and preaching second-hand sermons, but it is you who are the sinners, not me. There's Major, bossing everyone, pretending to be religious. Why, he's not a major, only a second lieutenant, and what's more he did not come to Iceland to be a missionary. He came to meet a girl, so there."

"Try one of these *venarbrauds*, Ingolf. They are smashing, like puff pastry with cream custard inside and icing on top. I got them in Reykjavik yesterday, that's why they've gone a bit mushy."

Jim was trying to change the conversation, but once Peter's temper was roused, it was a flaming fire.

"You needn't interfere, Jim James. If it hadn't been for your hideous yellow beard, there wouldn't have been all this mix-up. You've caused all the trouble. And Major is a bullying cruel brute, chasing a poor, half-starved deserter across half the world. I know all about how he witnessed against his own batman, and got him sent to prison. . . ."

Major had ignored the first insult. He now laid down his binoculars, through which he had been studying the flight of a golden plover.

"What do you mean by that, Ingolf?" he asked. "Who told you about the batman?"

Suddenly as it had flared up, Peter's rage subsided. He knew that he had betrayed the miserable fellow who had begged him not to tell Mr. Lang that he was in Iceland. He sat on the flowery bank, plucking at the blossoms, afraid to answer, for fear of letting out any more, painfully conscious that those piercing eyes of Major's were studying his face, reading in it what he wanted to hide.

Robert got out the spirit lamp and boiled water for the tea. They ate without any of the usual flow of conversation. Jim fingered his yellow beard, murmuring something about making his brother to offend. After tea, Jim and Major rode off together.

Robert, kindly as ever, packed up the tea-things and collected the horses.

"Don't be too hard on Major," he said. "He appears stern, but he is the kindest fellow in the world. When he decided to follow Christ, he had to make another decision which was not easy for him. The lady you saw this morning is very lovely and yet she is not a Christian. Moreover she is bitterly opposed to all who follow Christ. There can be no true love between a man and a woman whose lives are built up on different foundations. In order to serve his Master fully, Major had to give up more than you can imagine."

"Well, didn't he follow her to Iceland?"

"Indeed not. If he had known she would be here, he would not have joined our cruise. The colonel is a keen fisherman, and he happens to have chosen to spend his leave fishing over here. Don't jump to wrong conclusions."

Peter scowled. He remembered how quick Major had been in coming to his rescue in the river, and he did not want to be reminded of that misadventure. He was not now sure any longer that he was not a sinner. The place of the law had had an unpleasant effect.

Robert looked at his watch. "I'm going to alter our plans," he said, and then he called through cupped hands: "Coo'ee! I've changed my mind, chums. We will not visit the three farms, but go straight to the one where we spend the night.   There will be a gathering of people there so we shall have one meeting.   Tomorrow we will make for the main road and take the bus straight to Akureyri.   I think this riding is rather hard going."

Peter stiffened, angry once more.   So Robert thought he was tired and couldn't make it, did he?   The Northern Party had already changed its arrangements once for his benefit, now they must alter them again.   Peter Porter had spoiled the campaign.

Chapter 8

THE MOUNTAIN FARM

THE farm where they were to sleep was not nearly so comfortable as the one where they had lunched. Instead of a tidy wooden house with electric light and wide sunny windows, this was a farm built of turf and stone, three narrow cottages joined together with grass growing thickly on the roof, where a friendly goat was roaming. Behind, a wall of rock rose sheer and precipitous. In front there was a clump of rhubarb and a red-currant bush, by way of garden, and several neatly fenced fields, one of which contained a thin crop of barley. A woman came to greet them, accompanied by two small girls who stared round-eyed at the visitors, and then buried their shy faces in their mother's apron.

"*Verid ther saelar!*" said the woman courteously, and she sent the children to find her husband. She spoke no English, but the man of the house knew a little and he explained that David's friend had told them of their coming, and asked them to collect any neighbours who would like to hear the Word of God preached that evening. The interpreter was coming in his car, and several others would be along soon. Would the gentleman be so kind as to share a meal with them? This was the bedroom they could offer for their sleeping.

Peter shrugged his shoulders, resigned to face the worst. Never had he imagined that he would have to sleep in such discomfort. Camping out was a different matter. Nobody expected a soft bed in a tent. But to ride all those miles and then to land in a dive like this, it was preposterous! They were to sleep in what must have been used as a family junk room, a dark low place, the third of the three narrow cottages, which had a door leading to the mountain path, and a slit-like window. Another door connected with the big kitchen, which was also the family bedroom. Beyond the kitchen was the stable, with an emaciated cow and two horses. What a hovel!

Hovel or not, the kitchen was immaculate. Fresh, clean and furnished with excellent taste. There was an oil-painting on the wall, the work of the farmer, a really beautiful picture of the sunlit mountains, bright with their carpet of mosses, gold, and russet, and vivid green. Books there were in abundance, and a wireless set, and a piano. These isolated country folk were not without culture.

Salmon, skyr, eaten with hard sour red-currants, and the inevitable coffee and pancakes made a delicious supper after which Peter decided to go to bed. He had had enough of meetings and was sleepy. There was only one bed, and it would be greedy to bag that. One person must sleep on a sofa, covered in faded red plush, another must doss down on two chairs put together, and the fourth must make do with a pile of sheep-skins on the floor. Peter decided upon the two chairs, a choice which gave the impression of a most worthy unselfishness, leaving the bed and sofa for his elders, yet not choosing the floor for himself, where rats and mice might run over his face at night. The woman then took an enormous eiderdown like twenty pillows put together and stuffed it into a clean linen case. This would do duty for sheets, blankets and everything. Curled up on his chairs he could see in the dim light of the shadowy room piles of skins, an old loom for weaving the wool, a spinning-wheel and a lot of coats hanging by the door. He did not care about that door leading out to the bare mountain path. It was unlocked, but the farm people did not worry that there was no key. Iceland was an honest place, they said. The farm was too far from the road to attract thieves.

He heard people ride up on ponies and come indoors chattering and laughing. He heard the rain come tumbling down, and the night wind rising. He heard the clink of cups, as the Ice-landers shared their coffee. Then he heard singing, not the cheerful songs beloved of Jim James, but sad, slow music known to the Icelanders. Jim had a turn presently and enlivened proceedings considerably. He was using his mouth organ to-night, the accordion not being very tuneful after its swim in the sea. Peter stuffed his head beneath the eiderdown, trying to forget that Jim had given his other musical instruments to the Eastern and Southern parties, never thinking that anyone would be so beastly as to destroy his accordion. . . . A generous bloke, Jim. Fancy him giving Cherry-Garrard to Jon, too.

The music stopped and Robert spoke, translated by the interpreter. He began by reciting an Icelandic hymn in English. It was short and easy to remember:

> " Son, silver, sheep, when they
>   All lost and wandering were,
> Father, wife, herd, straightway
>   To seek and find did fare.
>
> In mercy so God's Son
>   Bears rich and ready aid;
> By each repentant one
>   God's angels glad are made.
>
> A son, a silver coin
>   of price, a sheep of Thine
> Make me, my Lord divine."[1]

"I expect he got that out of his book of translations of Icelandic hymns," thought Peter. "I like that one. I shall read it again."

"When we sailed into Reykjavik," said Robert,

---

[1] Translated from the Icelandic by W. G. Green.

"we passed the entrance to the Whale Fjord, where the writer of that hymn spent the last years of his life. As I gazed on those purple mountains and the deep sapphire waters of the fjord, I listened to an Icelandic friend telling me the life-story of Hallgrimr Petersson. You, my friends, know that story so well, but to me it was new. It is a story which reaches the hearts of all men, of whatever nation, for it tells how Jesus Christ, the Good Shepherd, sought and found the lost son, the lost coin, the lost sheep."

Half sleepy and yet wanting to hear, Peter listened as Robert went on to tell how the Icelandic boy Hallgrimr grew up within sound of the bells of the cathedral church of Holar, and how, knowing the truth of the love of God and the great salvation prepared for him, he yet decided to leave home and go his own way. Evil companions corrupted him and he drifted into sin, until the day came when the language of Hallgrimr Petersson was a byword for its vileness.

"It is not a good up-bringing that saves a soul, nor the environment of Christian people," said Robert. "Only Jesus Christ, the Lamb of God, can take away the sin of the world. Hallgrimr was rescued from his evil ways by a Christian man, and he was brought once more into the joyous fellowship of the Church of Christ, but again he went astray and fell into such sin that his life seemed ruined. But God was seeking him, as the father in the parable sought the prodigal son; as the woman sought her lost coin; as the shepherd sought his wandering sheep. Through disgrace, through remorse, through poverty, through the agonizing suffering of leprosy God sought him, until Hallgrimr Petersson brought himself, his sin and shame to the Crucified Saviour and found peace. From that broken life God made a radiance which has shone throughout Iceland for three hundred years."

Peter raised himself on his elbow, listening as the young curate explained how God can use any life yielded to Him. "Rebels who have fought against the heavenly King; deserters who have left His cause, careless ones who have ignored the wondrous love, the lost who wander despairing and alone, all can find pardon and peace by returning to Him who made them, who died to save them and who lives, interceding for them in Heaven.

"The fifteenth chapter of St. Luke's Gospel tells the three stories of Hallgrimr Petersson's lovely hymn, which we can make our prayer tonight:

> " A son, a silver coin
> of price, a sheep of Thine
> Make me, my Lord divine."

The interpreter translated Robert's words, and Peter moved to lie down again. The high puffy eiderdown slipped and he reached out to pull it back. As he did so a cold draught of air blew towards him. The back door leading to the mountain was open. The night was late, but summer nights in Iceland are never dark. Only it was dim in the low crowded room, and Peter had to screw his eyes to see who it was who stood there by the hanging coats and the bundles of luggage belonging to the far-farers.

The door opened farther and a man moved quietly out. Then the sheltering mountain hid him from view, but that thin figure and drooping head had made Peter wake up completely.

"That's Major's deserter. What was he doing? He must have come in while they were singing, or I would have heard him. I wonder if he stood listening there. . . . He didn't notice me, hidden under this bolster. Fancy him turning up in this lonely, out-of-the-way cottage."

Rain beat against the door and the wind howled round the farm. In the next room the interpreter's voice droned on. Peter cuddled down beneath his mound of down.

"I must have imagined I saw someone. That fellow would not be strong enough to walk all the way from Reykjavik. He looked on his last legs. I've been dreaming."

In a few moments he was asleep, but far too soundly asleep for dreaming.

Chapter 9

ROAD TO THE NORTH

"WHEN we get well on the way," decided Peter, "I'll tell Robert that I want to be a son and a silver coin and a sheep. But I won't mention it just yet. I'm not quite sure yet."

The night's rain had cleared away and morning gleamed orange and golden over the swampy plain they had traversed the day before. A V-formation of geese flew out against the gold, honking as they went, leading the way northwards. But the Northern Party had to veer eastwards now, to go across country to the main road where they should catch the bus for Akureyri, and eastwards led towards the glacier, all silver and green and threatening.

Jim and Robert rode ahead talking together in earnest tones. Major remained behind at the farm, and only joined his party when they had been riding for at least an hour. The grim expression on his face did not invite conversation. He rode some way in the rear, with the pack-horses.

"Whatever can they be talking about?" Peter

wondered.   He kicked his horse's sides to spur old Grettir on, but he could not catch up the two in front.

"They can't still be cross about yesterday. They were quite all right at breakfast-time. What's up now?"

They passed some girls hay-making in a meadow near a small farm and stopped for a while. The girls had been at the meeting the evening before, so they ran home to fetch a big jug of frothy goats' milk for the strangers to drink. Then on they rode as before, no one taking any notice of Peter.

The wind from the glacier blew cold as they rode over a wide stretch of tundra, starred with yellow saxifrage and mauve silenas. A stony path led into a valley which sloped upwards through the mountains. They had to ride single file here, for the path ran beside a stream, rattling and bouncing over its rocky downhill bed. It was nearly midday when they came over the pass and began to descend towards the village where they were to leave the horses.

"When are we going to have dinner?" asked Peter at last.

"If you are hungry we will eat now." Robert unpacked the meal and they sat on the stony ground and ate without conversation.

"Of all the dumb animals, you are the worst. You have not said one word all morning. What's the matter?"

Jim James answered without his usual smile:

"We have been waiting for your explanation. What were you up to last night when we were having our meeting?"

"I was in bed, asleep." Peter was not going to tell them now that he wanted to be a son, a silver coin and a sheep. No fear, the time had passed and they were cross.

"Uncle Wilfred asked me to take you on our tour in Iceland and he told me you were mischievous and spoiled. If I had known you were a thief, I would not have let you come. I did not expect any relation of mine would turn out a thief."

"I'm not a thief. It was you who took my money, and not I who took yours."

"I have precious little left for you to take, what with cablegrams and transatlantic telephone calls, and repairs to the accordion. If you had taken my cash I would not have minded half so much. But there could be nothing more despicable than to steal from the kind folk who gave us such a grand welcome last night. They are not rich, yet they gave us strangers the best they had. It was a dirty trick to go sneaking off to bed pretending to be tired and then steal the money left in one of those old coats by the door. Major and Robert have refunded the money to the farmer, between them, but nothing can destroy the harm you have done. They will not be likely to forget how an English boy behaved when they were trustful and generous to him."

"But it wasn't me. I never stole anything. There was a man in the room during the meeting. I saw him go out when the interpreter was talking. It must have been him."

"You have just stated that you were asleep during the meeting. Which part of your story is true?"

Peter was in a fix and no mistake. He could have told them all about the Major's deserter, but that he did not wish to do. The poor fellow had begged him not to tell tales, and he had already let out more than he had intended. To stick to his story of the man in the back room, meant describing the ex-batman. To draw back would be as good as accusing himself.

"I was sleepy. I didn't see him properly. You can search me and see if I have got any money, if you don't believe me."

They did not search him. They continued to believe he was guilty, and he was unable to prove that he was not. When dinner was over they rode on, but this time Peter made no attempt to join the others. He rode in silence alone, hatching plans for a getaway.

"I'm not going to trail round Iceland on a preaching tour, being made to feel a sinner when I'm not. They are worse than I've ever been, suspecting me of things I haven't done, not believing my word, taking my money from me. Now they'll probably get me sent to some Icelandic reformatory and I'll never get away home. How can I get off this weird island without a penny to pay my fare? "

The British Consul would be no help now. British Consuls would surely be sticklers for honesty, and would not dream of helping a boy accused of theft.

" Akureyri is a port. I'll have to stow away on board some English ship. It isn't easy, but it's the only way."

The more he thought of it, the less he liked the idea. His experience on the trawler had showed him that ships did not possess any great number of hideable holes where a large and healthy lad might stow himself for a considerable time without being noticed. Besides, supposing he got sea-sick again? Or what if he died of starvation? But come what may, suffer as he undoubtedly would have to, his only course lay in finding a suitable ship and getting aboard as soon as possible.

At last they came to the road and left the lava wastes, the dusty desert tracks among the foothills of the purple mountains. The road at first was no more than a rough path, rutted by the stout tyres of hardy motor vehicles going to and from one of the farms. The people there were surly and unfriendly, the first who had not welcomed the far-farers, but they pointed out the best route and soon the village and the main road to Akureyri came in view. The pastor of the little church greeted them warmly and invited them into his parsonage for coffee and sweet cakes.

The bus came along presently, packed full, with no place for them but the step. It was a long, weary ride, and even Jim's usual high spirits failed. There was no singing on the bus to Iceland's northernmost city.

"Good! There it is, and it seems a decent sort of town." Peter peered down the mountainside as the bus began the descent and saw in the half light of a summer dawn a fairly large town, nestling on the hilly slopes on the far side of a fjord. An ultra-modern church stood on the hill above it, dominating the place, oddly attractive with its tall narrow towers. Below there were houses set in gardens. On the shores of the fjord he could see the harbour with plenty of shipping, a hopeful sign. A couple of seaplanes floated in the water, but Peter could not imagine there would be much opportunity of getting aboard either of them.

They did not go to an hotel, as they had originally intended. Instead they left the bus and tramped through the town to pitch a tent on the outskirts, by a small clump of birch trees. The hotel would have provided comfortable beds and a hot bath, but money was scarce now that the sum stolen from the farmer had had to be drawn from the funds. Major could no longer afford the cost of the hotel.

"I hate the lot of them," thought Peter as

he curled up in his sleeping-bag. "I didn't steal the cash. I wish I had." A few kronur would have helped on his escape considerably. Without funds he had to make preparations as best he could.

He shovelled into his pocket some of the corned beef they had for breakfast, and a couple of slices of bread and butter. They would help on towards feeding him during the voyage home. Jim said he had shopping to do and went off alone when they had packed up the tent again. Major elected to remain in the birch wood with the baggage and cook the dinner. He had notes to make in readiness for the meeting he was going to take at one of the churches in the town and he wanted a quiet time.

"You can come with me, Ingolf," said Robert. "I am going to visit the sailors in the harbour and take them some books and invite them to Major's meeting tomorrow."

This was excellent! Robert could not have suggested a better way of spending the morning. Now Peter would be able to visit the ships without appearing to be inquisitive. He could find a hiding place and make sure of the time of sailing, as well as investigating without difficulty the nationality of the crew and the likelihood of a sympathetic reception if he should chance to be discovered. He helped himself to a packet of biscuits from the camping stores and set off with Robert, completely satisfied with his plans.

Robert was a good companion too. He was
not stern as Major was, neither was he exuberant
like Jim. His manner since the disastrous night
in the mountain farm was not quite so friendly,
but he chatted in a normal way as they walked
along, making no reference to any suspicions he
might still hold about the theft of the farmer's
money.

They admired the pansies and tulips and mari-
golds in the gardens and discussed the woollen mill
and leather factories for making shoes and hand-
bags and gloves. They inspected the dairy, all
shiny white tiles, and the coffee-roasting plant,
and they went round to see the open-air swimming
pool, which had hot water, an excellent idea in a
cold place.

Then down to the water-front, where a freighter
was unloading cargo, and in next to no time
Robert was chatting with the captain of an Icelandic trawler, a wooden boat of about seventy
tons, stout and sturdy, but no use to Peter since she
was not bound for England. The freighter had
come in from Canada, and the coaler beyond from
the U.S.A. Several fishing boats were tied up
alongside the quay, but they were not big enough
to hide a rabbit in, let alone a boy of Peter's
size.

"Ready, Ingolf!" called Robert. "Come, follow me."

If only he had not used those words, Peter would
have been thrilled to see the Hull steamer beyond

the freighter. But Robert said just what Jesus had once said to another Peter by the fishing boats; just what Jesus had said once too to a man who hadn't the courage to leave all and follow Jesus. Two nights ago, Peter had been on the point of following Jesus, but he had drawn back. Of course he could blame the others for their mistaken idea that he was a thief, but that should not have stopped him from following Jesus. Jesus Christ who knew all things knew that Peter had not stolen the farmer's money.

The mate of the Hull steamer made friends at once with Robert, and showed them both all round his ship. It was a perfect dream for a stowaway. The crew was short-handed, so there would not be a lot of men hanging round without much to do, on the look-out for people who should not be aboard. There was a big hold so stacked with cargo that anyone who could insert himself between the cases might hide for weeks without fear of discovery. Moreover there was a convenient hatchway aft down which a boy could wriggle when no one was looking, and best of all the steamer was due to sail that evening.

"Good egg! I'll slip out of Major's meeting when everybody is busy and get aboard. What a piece of luck!"

Major met them in the town and confessed with a sarcastic grin that his dinner, like King Alfred's cakes, had got burned.

"There's a place here where we can get a fish

dinner though, so I've seen Jim and arranged that we should eat together."

He led them into a sunny restaurant with tables arranged like high pews in an old-fashioned church. Each table had a pot plant with red leaves on its blue and white check table-cloth, and there was a ginger cat on the window-ledge. They sat down and waited for Jim James.

Presently the shop door opened and a young man came in. He wore a big Icelandic sweater knitted with a pattern of fishes and ships' wheels in dark brown, just like the one Jim's mother had knitted specially for this trip, but this man was much younger than Jim James, and clean-shaven. His hair was golden, like Jim's, and his eyes crinkled up into a smile the same way. . . .

Jim James had shaved off his handsome golden beard, the pride of his vain young heart.

"Whatever did you do that for?" asked Peter.

"I'd do more than that if I thought it would help you. Why should I wear a beard if it makes trouble? I'm just as handsome without one."

He laughed cheerfully, and Peter knew that his plan of stowing away on the Hull steamer must go the way the beard had gone. If Jim James would give up his fine adornment, then Peter Porter could give up his own way.

"I want some money to buy stamps," he said. "I've written some letters to my people. I did not steal the farmer's cash, but I'd like to pay my share towards what it cost you, because I'm a far-farer too. Will you take the rest of what Major has got of mine? "

The fish dinner was the very best meal they had had.

Chapter 10

IN THE WILD LANDS

"I CALLED at the Post Office to see if any mail had been forwarded from Reykjavik," said Jim. "Ingolf gets the lot."

There were eight postcards for Peter. All the far-farers had thought of writing to him. He had a picture of the docks at Reykjavik from Skipper May, the great *geysir* going up in steam from Eric, an Icelandic hospital from Doc, horses drinking from a tarn in a lava field from Fred, a coloured picture of the Aurora Borealis seen over Faxa Bay from David, the statue of Leif Eriksson from Taffy, and that of Ingolf the first Norse settler from Jon. Handy-Andy had not been able to get hold of a picture postcard, so he made one himself, a delightful sketch of Jon's home, with Jon's sisters and their big dog Baldur playing outside.

Peter felt a bit of a worm when he thought how disagreeable he had been, when the far-farers had all tried to make him enjoy his trip. Still, things were looking up now, and he was quite popular once more with the Northern Party. He seized his overcoat to put it on before leaving the restaurant, and out tumbled the remains of his breakfast and the biscuits, purloined from the store to feed a would-be stowaway!

There was a horrid pause. Then Major stooped and picked up the food, handing it to Peter with his wry smile. Jim laughed and Robert tactfully took no notice.

"Come on, chaps. We must round up all the children of Akureyri this afternoon," cried Jim. "They won't think I'm Father Christmas any more now, so we must put our backs into the job. It's a pity I didn't think of catching a reindeer before I had my beard off, it would have been a splendid attraction for a children's meeting. Fare forth, far-farers!"

The children's rally in the park was the best thing they had done yet. Jim was a Pied Piper, collecting little Icelanders by the dozen and persuading them to teach him their hymns. They had a fine Icelandic pastor to preach this time, so Peter did not take in a word of the sermon, but he understood right enough when Jim James produced his squeeze box and called:

"What about 'Onward Christian Soldiers', do you know that hymn? What? You don't? An Icelandic Bishop used to speak of 'God's Battle'. You are in the battle, whether you think you are, or not. The point is, which side are you fighting on?"

Most of his audience did not understand Jim's English, but Peter knew that the challenge was

meant for him. He must be on one side or the
other. If he refused to fight for Christ, he would
be one of the enemy's soldiers.

"The far-farers think I'm a thief and a liar,
but I am going to serve Christ, whatever they
think," was his resolve.

They played games with some of the children
when the meeting was over, and Jim sent Peter
off to buy some sweets for the kids. He was not
sorry to have a chance of shopping, and hastily
shooed off some small fry who wanted to come
and help him.

There was a sweet and grocery shop he had
particularly noticed earlier in the day, and a
certain line of delicacy on which he had already
decided. He went out of the park, and wandered
round, searching for the road where he had
seen that shop. The town was not large, so he
found it without difficulty, spent with care the
exact sum he had been given and took a short cut
to the park.

But the short cut proved to be a very long
one. Down a side street, which backed on to
the gardens of neat wooden and corrugated iron
houses, there was a shabby car. Like all Icelandic cars it was strongly built, made for rough
roads and hard wear. This car had evidently
had a good share of both. Peter inspected it as
he came down the road, and decided that the
driver must be a learner, for he went slowly,
wobbling from side to side in the road. It drew

up a little ahead of him and as he came alongside the driver jumped out.

He was Major's ex-batman, the seedy-looking deserter, and he was seedier than ever, a positive wreck, Peter thought.

"D'you mean to say you've come along here after me?" the man demanded. "So it's true then that Mr. Lang has been asking the police if they know where I am? You little spy, telling him I was about, informer, that's what you are."

Peter tried to pass, but without success. The man blocked his way. It was no use shouting, for there was no one to be seen but some very small children playing in the distance.

"Don't tell me you didn't say you'd met me," jeered the man.

It was true. Peter, in his rage, had let out the secret, enough at least to arouse Major's curiosity.

"Take that then!" The blow came so suddenly that Peter had no time to get away. He tried to avoid it, slipped on the rough paving and fell heavily, his head striking against the low garden wall.

When he came to his senses he was lying in the back of the shabby car. He gazed round him wondering what had happened. Yes, there was the deserter at the wheel, muttering to himself as he drove. What springs the car must have, for it bounced up and down as if it were being driven over rough country. Peter sat up, his head aching and his mouth dry and unpleasant.

There was no sign of Akureyri. The birch woods had gone. Larches, rowans, all had vanished. The fjord was no longer in sight. They were running over a desert, a rocky, water-less waste, edged with low, menacing black moun-tains. The sky was heavy and lowering above and the air was tinged with a smell like that of an experiment in the school laboratory, sulphuretted hydrogen or something of that sort, rotten eggs, everything that was horrible. A suitable place for a dragon's nest it was, but there was no sign of any living thing. The dragons must have turned themselves to stone, ages upon ages ago.

Slowly Peter's wits returned to him. The throb-bing in his head made it hard to think, but he knew that it was important to make no mis-take.

The man was ill, perhaps a bit mad. It would not do to annoy him. What Peter wanted to do more than anything was to jump out of the car which was moving slowly over the rubble. But that was the last thing he must allow himself to do, for there would be no help for him alone in that desert waste. Somehow he must persuade the man to drive him to safety, but which way did safety lie?

The driver went on mumbling and muttering, and the car lurched and swayed. Presently Peter began to make out the trend of the remarks in the front seat.

"I couldn't help it . . . didn't mean to kill the kid. . . . Many's the time I've had a clip on the lug and come to no harm. . . . How could I tell the boy would go over like that and bang his head on the wall? Dead, that's what he is, and it's my fault. . . . I couldn't help it. Haven't had nothing to eat for four days now. . . . What a feast I was going to have with that money I took from the farm, but I lost every bit of it, throwing the dice with that wog in Akureyri."

So he thinks he's killed me and he's hoping to bury my body in this wild place! It was not a pleasant thought.

"There's someone coming by those rocks. . . . I'll be caught, for sure. . . . No, it's only an old woman and a pony or two. . . . Coo! Thought I was done for then."

An aged woman tramped towards them, leading a pony by the bridle. A very aged man was riding the pony. He looked almost too old to sit astride, and he was propped up by bundles and what looked like a household removal. A second pony behind bore a tremendous load: bedding, chairs, a big washing basket stuffed with clothes; and the woman was also pushing a perambulator piled high with her treasures. In this weird desert the sight of anybody at all was surprising, but a family moving house was startling. The woman, however, was as much astonished to see the car and its occupants as they were to see her.

Stopping short, she waved and shouted, pointing and gesticulating. The deserter accelerated and drove on as fast as he dared on this uneven path.

"She's warning us not to go on this way," cried Peter, forgetting that he was supposed to be dead. The man jumped as if he had been shot.

"You've woken up then? I thought I'd done for you. Brought you for a ride and meant to tip out your body in some lonely spot and leave you there. Well, I guess I'd better do that just the same or you'll go telling tales again. I've no use for kids."

"Don't be daft. If you drop me out here, I'll soon put the police on you. Don't you know there's a telephone in almost every farm in this country? You'd better turn and go back."

"Back? Back again to Akureyri? Why, I don't know the way. We've been lost for over three hours. I got off the road and then I missed the path and it looks as if we shan't ever find it again."

Peter looked back uncertainly. It was not easy to see where they had come from. Over the dust-strewn plain the car-tracks were clearly visible here and there, but steering round countless rocks and avoiding cracks and fissures in the ground made their wake appear like a game of snakes and ladders.

Then quite suddenly the wheels of the car churned through the black sandy powder of the lava dust and stopped dead. There was no fuel left. She had run dry.

The man sat down on the running-board and held his head in his hands.

"Save yourself, kid," he groaned. "I'm done in. I've been ill these many days now. . . . I've lost count of time. I stole a passport from one of the crew in the boat I was on, and thought I'd be able to get a job over here, but I can't manage the lingo. . . . They soon tumbled to it that I was on the run. I hitched a lift part of the way to Akureyri when I heard Mr. Lang was in Iceland, and I managed to steal a bit of cash one night at a farm, but some gamblers took it the next day . . . fool that I was to risk it. . . . I thought I'd stow away aboard a ship in Akureyri, but the police there came asking who I was . . . Mr. Lang had told them to look out for me. They'll get me in the end now I've stole this car."

"You'd better have a sweet," said Peter. "They are not mine, but the chap they belong to would be sure to give you some if he was here. They are a foreign sort, but pretty good."

He sampled one and the deserter took one too. It was night now, a lurid queer sort of night, not dark, but far from light. The distant line of mountains was hidden in a mist. Around them the rocks took on the aspect of creatures turned to stone, prehistoric dinosaurs, iguanodons, pterodactyls, all the horrible animals that were found in that book of Conan Doyle's. Peter wished he had not borrowed it from the school library, but comforted himself with the reflection that in *The Lost World* the creatures were alive. Here in Iceland they never had lived.

"I can see some smoke over there," said the man. "Sure as my name's Bert Jones, that's a cottage of sorts."

"Come on, let's go and ask them to put us up for the night."

"You go, kid. Keep an eye on the smoke, and you won't get lost again. I'm staying here. My legs won't carry me any farther."

To walk alone to that cottage through the weird rocks was creepy to say the least, but the man would probably die if help was not soon forthcoming. Peter clenched his teeth and set off. After nearly an hour's scrambling, climbing, descending, and tumbling around the rocks, he came to his journey's end. There was no cottage. It was steam, not smoke, they had seen in the distance, and it poured up from mud craters in the earth, smelling so strongly of sulphur that Peter almost choked. He peered down one of the smaller craters, and jumped back as boiling mud and lava bubbled up towards him. The sun was coming up through the mist, though she had barely set a few minutes earlier. With a feeling of distinct pride Peter took out Cyril's camera and set the focus for one of the most extraordinary pictures which could possibly be presented for his school's photographic display.

"If it comes out, dawn over a place like this should win first prize if the colours come out. I'll call it 'Dawn over the Sulphur Springs in Ultima Thule' . . . sounds good, whatever it means. I heard Major call Iceland 'Ultima Thule' one day, and if it had been anyone else I'd have asked what it meant."

He stepped cautiously away from the hot springs. The soil round the crater was tinged with glorious shades of copper, blue and rose-pink, but it had a hollow feeling as if it was just a thin crust which might collapse at any moment beneath his weight.

Bubble! Bubble! The mud gurgled and steamed. Peter retreated, remembering suddenly that he had come to find a cottage and to get help for Bert Jones. And there was no cottage and no help. He had wasted too much time already.

Drearily he turned back and made his way to the car. He could see his way better now, for the sun was dispersing the mist, but the lurid midnight dawning was uncanny, and the odd shadows that lurked round those rocks tripped him several times, so that he scraped his hands and knees, tore his trousers and banged his forehead. By the time he reached the car, he was black with lava dust and very weary. No answer came when he shouted to Bert Jones.

On the front seat, slumped over the wheel, was the deserter, lying in a dead faint. Now it was

Peter's turn to find himself apparently alone with a dead fellow-traveller.

For a moment he panicked. Then he remembered. He was not alone; the Lord who sought the lost ones was near at hand. Standing in the powdery black dust by the car, he repeated the Icelandic hymn:

> " Son, silver, sheep, when they
>   All lost and wandering were,
> Father, wife, herd straightway
>   To seek and find did fare.
>
> In mercy so God's Son
>   Bears rich and ready aid;
> By each repentant one
>   God's angels glad are made.
>
> A son, a silver coin
>   of price, a sheep of Thine
> Make me, my Lord divine."

H

Chapter 11

THE BLACK RIVER

ON his way back, he had passed a small brackish pool of water. It was not fit to drink, but he poured some over Bert's head and gradually brought him round. Then helping him to lie down on the back seat, he stretched his own coat over him and settled down himself in the front of the car. It was no good doing anything until morning came. The midnight sun was all very well, but one gets tired and useless after twenty-four hours awake. Some more of the sweets helped to ward off starvation, and before long they were both sound asleep.

A roar like that of a distant cannon brought Peter to his feet and made Bert Jones wake up and roll over. Outside the car it was quite dark.

"But it isn't night. The sun came up again while I was away over there by the *geysirs*. Whatever is the matter?"

"It's a dust storm, like they have out east," said Bert Jones.

Another roar, and a huge mushroom-shaped cloud rose above one of the distant mountains.

"It's an atom bomb!" yelled Peter.

"Garn! Iceland don't have no atom bombs. She don't need 'em. She's got enough hydrogen in her insides to blow up the world without going to the trouble of splitting atoms. I tell you what that is, it's a volcano taking off."

Peter whipped out Cyril's camera. Dawn breaking over a steam-filled *geysir* colony was nothing to be compared with a volcano in eruption. Coo! What would the chaps at school say to this? The geography master would go crackers!

"Hey there, look out, kid. See the lava pouring down the mountainside, like a black river it is. And there's dust blowing right over here . . . and it's not dust, lad. It's cinders! Run for your life!"

They ran both together, madly, blindly, aiming only for the opposite side of the world from that flaming horror behind them. Fear lent strength to the man who had been so ill last night, and fear spurred on Peter Porter to struggle over all obstacles, rocks, loose sand, pot-holes, and slippery scree. Presently they came to a change of scenery, where the wild lands were broken by peaks and pinnacles of rock, mostly about the same height, some cone-shaped, others round on top. Some stood jagged like broken teeth and some were beautiful in a strange way, like the pillars of a ruined colonnade. The ground between was all thick with grey lava dust, but the rock shapes hid from them the petrified sea they had crossed. When they looked back they could see no longer the black ash cloud or the snaky form of the lava river pouring down from the fiery mountain. They could not see, but they knew soon it would overtake them, swirling round through the peaks and pinnacles, and engulfing the weary runners before they could reach safety.

"Come on," gasped Peter, but there was no reply to his urging. He looked back. Bert Jones had slumped over again and lay in a heap on the ground.

"I don't know which way to go. We may be running round in circles. I must stop and find out where we are."

Peter's breath came in gulps; his heart pumped furiously. Standing still made him notice the stitch in his side. He longed to throw himself on the ground and rest, but even a few moments' pause might bring destruction to them both.

There was a big rocky pinnacle in front of them, one of the rounded kind, not too difficult to climb. Perhaps from the top he would be able to see a cottage or a roadway, something to guide them, somewhere to find help.

No cottage was in sight, but something far more welcome. Standing on top of another rounded rock pinnacle was a man, searching the landscape through binoculars. The erect straight figure, so cordially detested, was the most welcome sight in the whole world.

"Major!" bawled Peter, waving his arms and

Cyril's camera. He could have shouted with joy at the sight of the man he had hated. Major waved back and called, then sprang down from his rock and ran towards Peter.

"Bert, Bert, wake up. It's all right. Major's here. We're saved!" He shook the unconscious man, and then set off at a run, shouting and then listening for Major's answer.

"Where's Jones?" was all the greeting he got.

"By the rock where I stood. He's dying, I think. He can't move and the lava is coming that way."

"I'll fetch him. Walk towards those three peaks together. Don't run or you'll not reach them. Jim James is behind them with a car. Be careful."

Major darted off and Peter dragged himself towards the three peaks. He was far too weary to think of running now, and the distance seemed like a hundred miles, all uneven and crevassed as it was.

But behind the peaks there was a green oasis, a stretch of grass and bright green moss with a stream trickling through. And there was Jim James turning a car with the help of an Icelander who waved his arms in welcome.

"What-ho, Blackamoor!" cried Jim. "All the hot springs in Iceland won't wash you clean! Now we must send out a search party to find Major."

"He's gone to fetch the batman." Peter sat down suddenly on the grass, his legs giving way beneath him. He could not say any more. The thought of that black river seeping on towards Major and his batman blotted out everything else from his mind. He had hated and insulted Major and he had despised Bert Jones, and now what was happening to them away among the rock peaks?

The Icelander produced a flask of hot sweet coffee and poured out a lidful for him. The volcanic dust blew into it, but the hot drink pulled Peter round again. It was wonderful to hear Jim James rattling on in his old way:

"With your permission, I'll just take a photograph of you sitting there, black as a gramophone disc, with an erupting volcano for a background. Our friend Arnor here says that old Askja has about finished for today, and she may not break out again for a thousand years, so this is our last opportunity of seeing her show off. Feeling better now are you? Good."

"Where's Robert?" asked Peter anxiously, as a whirl of pumice cinders landed around them.

"He's having a sea-trip. He got a notion that you had it in mind to stow away aboard a Hull steamer that you were mighty interested in, so he hired a motor-boat and went after her; a wild-goose chase, it appears. Meanwhile Major got the whole of Akureyri standing at attention, and before long he discovered that two small girls had seen a man knock you down and push you into a car. Being girls they had not observed what kind of car or where it went, but an old

dame telephoned from a farm out this way to say
she had seen a car with a man and a boy heading
towards the volcano. She and her husband were
scuttling out of danger, but they could not manage to stop you. Then Major organized the search,
and got hold of this brave fellow to drive his
taxi out here. Not the best part of the world to
get lost in. Needles in haystacks are nothing
beside boys in a lava desert."

"We were lost like the son and the silver and
the sheep, and Jesus sent you to find us. First He
found me, and then Major came."

Jim James whistled. A glad look came into
his merry face and his eyes crinkled up the way
they did when he was happy. He opened his
mouth and shouted at the top of his voice:

"Rejoice! Rejoice! Rejoice!"

The hills brought back the echo. Rejoice, rejoice, rejoice! Major must have heard it as he
stumbled through the cinders and dust. The
Icelander shrugged his shoulders, wondering what
these Englishmen were up to. Under the shelter
of a great rock, a half-conscious deserter heard it
afar off, and, looking up, he saw coming to help
him the man whom he had slandered and loathed.

Chapter 12

HOMEWARD BOUND

PETER sprang off the bus from Akureyri, and raced off to be first at the quay. There lay the old *Far-Farer*, rocking slightly at her moorings, her red sail set and her funnel smoking, all ready to put to sea when the tide turned. Peter's pack crashed on the deck and he jumped on board.

"Hey, Skipper, where are you? We're back!"

Through the hatch emerged a bald head, fringed with white whiskers.

"Do you together fare to be comin' aboard tonight then? It's a day late you are an' all."

"We were held up at Akureyri. A volcano erupted and I got lost and one of Major's soldiers who deserted nearly died in the lava plains. We had to leave him in hospital."

"You've had a prarper owd time, you have. What'll you take for supper?"

"Anything, so long as there's plenty of it. Where's David and Taffy?"

Skipper May whistled through his fingers and the two appeared, Taffy from the engine-room

and David from the galley.   All four talked at
once there was so much to say, but bit by bit
the news of the Western and Northern Parties
leaked out.

"Man, we had a grand time at Akranes, such a
gathering and a message that many will never
forget!   And Keflavik, Ingolf, the Americans
there, we got 'em all in . . . ."

"Robert went to look for me in a motor boat,
but he went too far north and crossed the Arctic
Circle.   The boatman said he'd lost his charts. . . ."

"So Robert is the only one of us to win the
Order of the Blue Nose, is he?   We'll invest him
with the insignia when he comes along."

"Ingolf, did you see the Godafoss where the
heathen Icelanders threw their gods into the
water?"

"No, but I got some lovely snaps of the eruption
—if they come out."

"I reckon 'at we'd better goo down and begin
supper. . . ."

"Come on then.   What's to eat?"

Steaks and onions and a Christmas pudding out
of a tin welcomed the returning far-farers. Robert
and Jim came in time for the festive meal but
Major only turned up when everything was
finished.   He had driven from Akureyri with one
of the hospital doctors, for he had stayed with Bert
Jones until the last minute.   He spread butter
and jam thickly on a hunk of bread and poured
himself out a mug of tea.

"The doctor says Jones is recovering, but he has had a bad time. Poor fellow! He is quiet now and has found peace, but he will have to face the music when he gets back. I think though that the experience he has gone through may make a man of him. There's the stolen money and the stolen passport and the stolen car to account for, as well as desertion and landing here under false pretences. That chap was once a Christian, years ago. He went wrong in the Army and deserted in two ways. Thank God now he has come back to fight on the right side in God's Battle."

"I went to see him before I left," said Peter. "He told me that I was wrong when I said you were a beastly hard character. Of course I had found out by then that you weren't, but Bert Jones said to me, 'Good-bye, kid, and don't forget we were both wrong. Mr. Lang is strict, but he is a Christian man. A Christian didn't ought to be a pussy-cat.'"

"It do be getting late," said Skipper. "If you are ready, sir. . . ."

Robert stood up and from his pocket there fell a bundle of letters. He had collected them from the Post Office and forgotten to give them out.

With a characteristic yell, Jim James pounced upon the top letter, a blue air-mail letter card addressed to:

Peter Porter Esq.,
 L/T *Far-Farer*,
  Reykjavik Docks,
   Iceland.

"Peter Porter. . . . This is addressed to Peter Porter. . . . It can't be meant for you, Ingolf, can it?"

His voice trailed away into nothing. He stared at the letter and then at Peter, then at another addressed to himself.

"That's me, it must be Uncle Bill at last . . ." said Peter.

But it was not Uncle Bill's writing. His fingers wobbled as he tore it open. Before he had time to read it, there was a heavy groan from Jim James, who sat down, his head buried in his hands, and then rose, bowing majestically to Peter.

"Peter Porter, my friend, a thousand apologies, ten thousand in fact. I too have had a letter. My excellent Uncle Wilfred, my miserable Cousin Cyril and my deplorable self, we have between us kidnapped an unfortunate youth and worse than that; we have caused you to be blamed as a lying rascal, pitied as a split-minded schizophrenic, scolded as a troublesome nuisance.

"Friends and far-farers, allow me to introduce to you Peter Porter, no relation whatever to me. Listen while I read aloud a letter from my uncle, who is also the great-uncle of Cyril Copeland, the

boy who should have accompanied us on our
tour."

They sat round the cabin table listening as
he read the letter:

"Dear Jim,

My niece and I have been much worried
since hearing from you. Your suggestion that you
might have taken the wrong boy did not at first appear
possible. Of course you have not seen Cyril since he
was two years old, so you would not know what he is
like now, especially as you were only seven at the time
yourself. We thought of course that your telephone
conversation meant that Cyril was up to mischief—
acting again. But now we have had sufficient proof
that Cyril did not in fact join you on your trip to Iceland. He is a very naughty boy indeed, and merits
severe punishment. He must have induced some
other lad to exchange places with him and he has
spent a week on the Broads on a cruise for schoolboys, at the end of which he went home with one of
the participants and stayed for another week in a
Rectory in Devon. I am glad to say that the Rector
discovered what Cyril was up to and has informed
me.

"Of course by now you will have investigated the
other boy's claims and you will certainly have informed
his parents of this disgraceful plot.

"I have punished Cyril most severely. His mother is
distressed but I feel sure I have acted for the best. He
is deprived of pocket-money, ices and sweets for a week,
during which time he will go to bed early, at 8.30 p.m.
This will be a real hardship. . . ."

Everyone laughed at that and Major said:
"A good thrashing would have more effect.

Peter Porter, did you or did you not arrange this exchange with Cyril Copeland?"

"I never saw Cyril Copeland in all my life. I don't know him."

"Then how did he find out that you were going to the Broads?"

Peter related all over again the story of Mavis and her paper boats made out of the letter Father had hardly read; the instructions half remembered about a bearded man to be met at Ely, and Jim James who had suited the description so well.

"But, you young idiot, I told you about our trip to Iceland as we drove along. Why did you not say one word to explain that you were to sail on the Broads?"

"I didn't listen. You talked about church architecture and I wasn't interested. You never stopped talking, but I stopped listening. Then we passed Oulton Broad, and I thought that was where we were going."

"Perhaps your letter will explain," said Robert.

Peter unfolded his letter and read it aloud:

"Dear Peter Porter,

You were a chump not to see what I was up to in the train. Fancy sitting opposite to an old lady who kicked you on the shins and never guessing that an old woman would not wear boys' shoes! The bearded man your Dad told you to meet guessed at once when I kicked him. Chased me all round Ely he did after I'd seen you going off with my second **cousin once removed, Jim James**, whose photograph I have seen, though I don't know him. I saw your name on your luggage, but no address, and your Dad said meet the bearded man, so I went up and said, 'I'm Peter Porter' and kicked him. . . . He caught me near the Cathedral with half Ely in pursuit. He seemed a decent sort, so I decided I'd let you go for a cruise with a gang of religious types and I'd have the schoolboys on the Broads. I wrote twice to your uncle, old black-beard had his address, and I had a lovely time. I have learned to swim, caught two eels and I can sail a wherry. You must have been pretty dull, being the only young one in the trawler, sea-sick too most likely. Hard luck! Have your wits about you next time you go travelling.

"The snag about the Broads was that one of the chaps invited me home afterwards and his Dad found out. . . . A nice chap, his Dad, a parson, so I have had to revise my opinion of religion. Not, mind you, that I am going to turn out like my exemplary Cousin Jim, who is always held up to me as a young saint, but I'm keeping an open mind on such matters. The bearded schoolmaster too was a Christian, but I kept out of his way after the first day. He had a sense of humour, but he would not have approved of what I'd done . . . besides, now I hear that Uncle Wilfred has decided to send me to the school where he teaches so I fear it's all up with me.

Yours truly,

CYRIL COPELAND.

"So my Cousin Cyril was that old lady who behaved so badly at the railway station. I ought to have guessed."

"He vowed he'd cause you a lot of trouble if he had to come. Well, so he did, or I did. But I'm glad I came, even if I haven't caught two eels or learned to sail a wherry. I've seen a volcano erupt and I've been kidnapped and lost, and I've seen hot springs and Thingvellir and most of Iceland too, and best of all I'm a real far-farer now, not just a mistake."

"Six months ago," said Jim, "I was sitting in my rooms in Teddy Hall, poring over Thorvald's Saga, unable to make head or tail of it, when in came Jon, whom I had met when he was staying with friends in North Oxford. He helped me with the translation, and suddenly some words seemed to stand out from the page:

"Faro their vida um Island at boda Guds ord.

"'Far fared they round Iceland to preach the Word of God.' Those old Viking missionaries were called the far-farers, and I said to myself, far-farers, why not today? We set out, brothers, to win Icelandic people for the Lord, and we fared all round Iceland to win two of our own countrymen. Praise God. His word is never preached in vain."

"Do an' you together don't get singin' now, us'll have to put to sea without," called Skipper. Jim James seized his accordion and they tumbled up on deck.

Over the quayside, across the sleeping town, out to the wide bay and away to the tossing ocean waters rang the singing from the far-farers in the Lowestoft trawler.

" Oh the deep, deep love of Jesus!
Spread His praise from shore to shore.
How He loveth, ever loveth,
Changeth never, nevermore."

Then quietly the *Far-Farer* slipped from her moorings and set her course homewards.